A Lovely
Monster

THE ADVENTURES OF CLAUDE RAINS
AND DR. TELLENBECK

A NOVEL

Rick De Marinis

Simon and Schuster New York

DESIGNED BY IRVING PERKINS
MANUFACTURED IN THE UNITED STATES OF AMERICA

1   2   3   4   5   6   7   8   9   10

LIBRARY OF CONGRESS CATALOGING IN PUBLICATION DATA

DE MARINIS, RICK.
    A LOVELY MONSTER.

    I. TITLE.
PZ4.D3742LO[PS3554.E4554]   813'.5'4   75-22199
ISBN 0-671-22175-2

For Carole

I come prepared, unwanting what I see,
But tied to life. On the royal road to Thebes
I had my luck, I met a lovely monster,
And the story's this: I made the monster me.

The Approach to Thebes

TELLENBECK SAID a pain word out loud while going over
the TV schedule. He said he was sorry. I could see that
he was. He promised me a new coloring book, a new box
of crayons, and will now let me watch TV until eleven
P.M. and that is good of him, but, even so, I cannot stop
crying.

My hands are delicate. The skin is almost transparent.
The bone is brittle. The heart pumps, pumps, pumps,
but where is the blood? The hands are cold, and the
blood is not there. I have told Tellenbeck to turn the
thermostat up, but he says, *Claude, it's on eighty already.*
Turn it up to ninety, then, I tell him, and he does. Tellenbeck is good to me. He sits on my bed and pats my
hand. "You are not *brittle*, Claude," he says. "It's all in
your mind. You must learn not to be so morbid."

The pain word stays in my head as if just spoken and
I cry. Why does it stay?

"I'm truly sorry, Claude," says Tellenbeck. And he is.
I know it. I try to blow my nose but I am afraid to touch
it. It feels brittle in my brittle fingers. Tellenbeck takes
his own handkerchief and wipes the trickle with it. "We
must always be concerned with pulmonary embolism,
the last hurdle," says Tellenbeck. "There is light at the

end of the tunnel, laddybuck," he says. "Rome wasn't built in a day."

I named myself. Alpha Six means I am the sixth of an experimental series called Alpha. But that is not a name. Tellenbeck referred to me as *Alph* in his notes for a while but I would not respond to it verbally. The experiment is over: Call me Claude. Tellenbeck would say, *How are your jonquils doing, Alph?* and I would not answer him. My jonquils were doing fine. I water them every day from my bed. I talk to them and soon they will bloom for me. Later, when my strength comes, I will be able to plant new bulbs outside in the fresh air and light. But I would not answer to that nomenclature. Because that is what it is. Like V-I for the Buzz Bomb, or Saturn III for the rocket, or Mark-9 for the six-slice toaster. I am not a machine with nomenclature. No. I am a Person. Claude.

Claude Rains, after the actor Claude Rains, whom I admire very much and wish to emulate. I watch all his movies when they appear on TV. I watch all the other movies too. Until Tellenbeck turns the TV off. I am glad he will now let me watch it until eleven P.M. It had been lights out at ten. *You need to sleep, Claude,* he said. *Sleep heals.* I watch the Early Movie, the Movie at Noon, and the Evening Classic of Yesteryear. Now I will be able to see one of the Network Movies too.

Thinking a pain word does not hurt. Only when it is spoken out loud does it bother me. I am making a list of them. So far there are more than fifty. I add the latest one to the list and give it to Tellenbeck to memorize. The sound pierces something deep behind my ear and he must memorize them and not say them ever in my presence.

Clabber. Number fifty-seven. Tellenbeck said, "The drama is a clabber of sound and fury, signifying far too much." He was reading from the TV schedule about one of Claude Rains's last movies. The TV schedule did not recommend the movie. The TV schedule was in error.

Claude Rains, experiment six, Monster. Monster. I call myself that because that is what I am. I do not mind. The noun is correct and it is not a nomenclature. Tellenbeck does not approve of the word. "Please, Claude," he says. "Don't use that word." It is a fear word.

"But it is accurate, Doctor Tellenbeck," I answer.

"That's unfilial of you, Claude," he says, attempting to laugh at the joke we might be sharing.

"Do not patronize me, Doctor," I say, and he laughs with wonderful heartiness. I am learning humor.

"Neo-frankensteinian meta-man," I say, proud of my flawless syllabication. Tellenbeck makes his jaws tight with imagined agony. "The creature from the black lagoon," I say, and Tellenbeck puts his fist to his cheek and moans. It is amusing.

He would prefer that I use his first name, Kraft, but I do not feel able to at this time.

We might be watching TV and he will make up a

nice tray of snacks and bring it into the room, wanting me to say, *Thank you, Kraft*, but the words are not there, though I would like to be filial, because he has done so much for me, and where would I be today if it were not for him, but even so I cannot bring myself to do anything but nod, blink, or curl a finger into my ear, and say, *Thank you, Doctor Tellenbeck*, keeping my eyes all the while on the movie.

Last night it was *Captain Caution* and he brought one of my favorite snacks, endive and mayonnaise on whole wheat toast with pepper and salt and a glass of ginger ale on ice. "Thank you, Doctor Tellenbeck," I said. His face was sad, the agony in his jaws was not imaginary, the sudden distance in his eyes was real. I was sorry. He sat next to me on the bed. I ate the sandwich quickly, making sure to keep my lips together as I chewed and the noise of my teeth minimal. I felt bad. I thought: *What is wrong with me?* I took large bites and washed them down with large, tickling swallows of ginger ale. I put the tray in his lap. "More," I said, without gratitude. I felt bad. On TV a volley of cannon fire was directed against a sailing ship. While he was in the kitchen I said aloud, "Oxidize," to punish myself. *Oxidize* is number twelve on the list and underlined in red for it is one of the worst. I felt a nail being driven in behind my right ear. Tears rolled down my face. Tellenbeck did not see them when he came back into the room.

"Here you are, Claude," he said, so generous and kind, so watchful and good.

Sometimes I cannot converse with him for minutes. An embarrassment thickens the tongue. A sadness paralyzes the jaws. In such moments I sometimes mention the Fly. *He is back, Doctor Tellenbeck,* I will say—though he is never really gone—and point to the ceiling. Tellenbeck will fold a magazine in half and climb up on a chair and look at me for instructions. *Right above your head, next to the light fixture.* He looks but does not see it. *Here?* he asks. *A foot to your left, Doctor.* He swipes at the ceiling, missing by inches. The Fly moves to another spot. It is frustrating to watch from the bed. Tellenbeck slaps the ceiling with the magazine as if the Fly were still there. He never sees it. *Get down, Doctor,* I say. *It is gone.* It is metallic black and big as a wasp and yet he does not see it. I almost have to laugh.

I began blank. Sometimes something comes back. When it does I mention it to Tellenbeck. He says not to worry and carries me back into the workshop and focuses the biodrill on me and says to relax. He asks me what type of image it is. Sometimes it is very clear. A tree stump, a puddle of water in it, a trembling of leaves nearby, a Female, older than the rest, singing.

"Older than the rest?" Tellenbeck asks. "Who are the rest? Describe, please."

I do not know. I cannot describe. They are peripheral.

It is more a feeling than an image. A dull patch of light perhaps, a smell, a clicking of cold sticks or a choking mist. It is Someone Else's past. It is a puzzle.

"Well," says Tellenbeck, always cheerful, always kind, "we'll take care of it." He straps me down to the table and turns on the machine. I have to wear thick glasses which are black in color and a crushing jacket of lead. The biodrill hums and snaps and a needle of light touches my forehead. The biostrobe makes the room stagger left and right, and the walls bow. Later, Tellenbeck says, "Tell me about the tree stump and the woman singing and the others." It is not possible. I remember telling those things. But there is no picture. It is odd. There is nothing but the words, which are part of my own memory, a transference from the other, but even these are weak and changing and will, I know, soon be gone.

Tellenbeck says he is bringing me up to speed. I can do all the arithmetic operations easily. I am reading on the first-year college level. Even so, I like the Fables best of all which Tellenbeck read to me those first few weeks when all I could do was lie here and watch the ceiling where the Fly would sit and rub his front legs together and nod his horrible head until the tears filled my eyes and I could not see him any longer though he buzzed. Tellenbeck wants to stop. He says I am beyond the Fables. He thinks it is wrong for him to read them to me at night after TV. *You're a big boy now*, he laughs. Then I cry. Then he reads.

Some Fables disturb but Tellenbeck no longer reads these to me. My favorite is *Jack and the Beanstalk*. Not the part about the cow and the magic beans but the part about the castle and the magic goose.

The part about the giant Female and the part about the giant.

I now exercise. I sit up and move my arms outward and in and over my head. There is pain where the scar tissue is. It is healed but stiff. There are many scars. But they are narrow and the flesh was sealed with cellglue. Soon there will be no scars to see. Tellenbeck has told me so. He looks at them every day and shakes his head. *Marvelous*, he says. *Bloody marvelous*. Tellenbeck is a genius. He picks me up and carries me to the bath. I like it hot. The scars like the heat. I can feel the blood beating in them. I can feel the blood beating in my hands and feet, which are always cold. Tellenbeck washes me carefully. "Nothing scummier than a sickbed," he says. Soon I will not have to stay in bed all the time. "It looks like we're in the clear," Tellenbeck says. "Home free."

Sometimes I have the feeling that everything that is happening now has happened before. Tellenbeck says not to worry. It is a condition. It can be fixed. It is a touch of epilepsy. Some bruised cells in the temporal lobes. Nothing serious. I can have a pill for it or if it gets stubborn we can implant some electrodes. "A touch of epilepsy," says Tellenbeck, "is a small price. Just think of the other dreadful possibilities." Tellenbeck knocks on wood. He has me knock on wood. We knock on wood together. We do it often.

Sometimes Tellenbeck paces back and forth in my room and speaks into his recorder. "Everything can be retrieved," he says. These are his notes, his memos to posterity. "Not just fingers and eyes. Not just patches of skin and bits of bone. But brains and pieces of brains. Entire nervous systems and fragments. Energized, vitalized, pulsing, yielding and refusing to yield, devouring and refusing to be devoured, the whole buzzing universe of cells hugging the continuum of life. Total cellular compatibility will be the sunrise of a new era! Cell-mediated graft-rejection will be a forgotten specter of the past!" I do not like to listen when he records his voice. When he does, I count to one thousand by eights.

Tellenbeck has bought me new crayons. I like them when they are new. When they are old it is hard to stay within the lines. With new crayons it is easy. At first I would shake. The hand would jump, ruining the page. The crayon would cross the line. I would cry. I would pull the page out of the coloring book and tear it with my teeth. It was so frustrating. It was so difficult. *Patience, patience,* Tellenbeck would say and I would just look at him and he would pick up the book and the crayons and turn on the TV instead. But I am much better now. I have skill. I stay within the lines.

"That's not all I brought you, Claude," Tellenbeck

says. He leaves the room and returns with something large. It gleams in the sunlight from the window. "What is it?" I ask. I like surprises. I am excited.

"It's a collapsible wheelchair. It's high time we got you into the fresh air and sunshine."

He also has a large package with him. I like presents. But it may not be a present. "Yes," he says. "That's for you, too." He breaks the string. He pulls back the gray paper. "Clothes," he says.

Tellenbeck dresses me. "Going to deck you out, Claude," he says, sliding my thin arms into the sleeves of the shirt. The clothes are very pretty. Orange-and-black socks, white shoes, gray slacks, black shirt, white belt, a checkered cap. Sunglasses. "There," he says. "How you like, laddybuck?" He picks me up and holds me in front of the mirror. He lets my feet touch the floor. I am frightened. I grip his neck. My hands are losing their color, becoming transparent. The blood is pooling around my heart, refusing to move. I am brittle. "Easy, *easy*," he says. "I won't drop you, Claude." My arm is around his shoulder and his arm is around my waist. In the mirror we are standing side by side. My heart is pumping very hard, but where is the blood? My legs are trembling like the stems of my jonquils when the breeze from the air conditioner blows through them. I am afraid of my spleen. I am afraid of rupture. I am afraid of clotting in the arteries. I am afraid of major dysfunction. "Stop *worrying*," Tellenbeck says. "No sweat, keed. Everything's humming."

He puts me in the wheelchair and we leave the apartment. This is the first time.

I did not know we lived in such a beautiful place. It reminds me of the castle and the magic goose. The sky is crayon blue. The lawns are crayon green. "This is called a condominium," says Tellenbeck.

"Condo-minium," I say. There is no pain in the unfamiliar word.

"This is where we live," he says. There is water so clear and deep I feel an imbalance just to look into it. "That is the pool, Claude." He stops the chair. He squats down next to me. The sun is so warm on my legs. The air so sweet. The sky so bright. I see there are trees with flowers on the branches. There are vines with flowers. I am so happy.

There are others. "Those are called sunbathers, Claude," Tellenbeck says. They glisten like juicy meat in the pan. They make saliva fill my mouth. "Swallow, Claude," says Tellenbeck. A Female rises. She stretches her arms over her head and yawns. Her glands are very large and paper-white under the loosely held fabric, though her limbs are crayon brown. "Those are called tits," says Tellenbeck. His lips are close to my ear. I do not see her scars.

"Tits," I say. There is no pain in the unfamiliar word. Tellenbeck puts a finger to my lips. Am I expected to kiss? I am not able to at this time.

The sun is so warm I doze. The dream comes. I push the last leaves and branches aside and step into the meadow. The castle shines in the distance. It is a dream of walking. There is danger. There is pleasure. There is a sign. Do Not Enter. But I enter. The giant Female and the magic goose are in the room. "At last," says the giant Female. She picks me up and presses me against her Tits. They are warm and white. Her arms shine with golden oil. An egg slides out of the goose. The big clock ticks. Tick tock. The giant is out in the field. I hear him grunting. "The pig," says the giant Female. I see that she is afraid. I wonder if she is afraid of an infarction or spontaneous pneumothorax. She looks at me and touches my hair. Her scars are visible. "He ruptures me," she says.

"Fifteen minutes," says Tellenbeck, looking at his watch. I do not want to go inside yet. "We'll come out again tomorrow," he says. "We don't want to overdo it." I do not want to go inside yet. He sees that I am going to cry. "For Christ's sake, Claude," he says. Then I cry. "They're looking at you," Tellenbeck whispers into my ear. He sounds like the teakettle. "We don't want them to start asking difficult questions, do we?" I blow my nose.

A Sunbather bends down to look at me. "Anything wrong?" she asks. I see her Tits hanging down and between them there is a blazing patch of light.

"Nothing, really," says Tellenbeck, smiling.

"I have just learned that my mother has a liver dysfunction," I say. Tellenbeck looks at me. "The surgery is scheduled for the morning," I say. Tellenbeck squeezes my shoulder. "I am very worried," I say.

"I don't blame you," says the Sunbather. I wipe my tears. The Sunbather touches my hand. Tellenbeck pushes the chair.

"Where did you learn to fib like that?" says Tellenbeck when we are back inside.

"It wasn't a fib," I say. "It came into my head. Like the other times."

Tellenbeck looks worried. He takes my new clothes off and carries me into the workshop. He puts me on the table and turns on the machine. "What is your mother's name?" he asks.

"María Consuela Villareal de Abrigán."

He spins the dials and snaps the toggles.

I do not know where these things come from. Or where they go.

Tellenbeck says my strength is multiplying at a surprising rate. Today I stood. Tellenbeck does not know. I sat up. I let my legs slide out of the bed. I let my feet touch the floor. My toes went into the coarse polyester shag. A sickness in my stomach came and went. There were spots larger than eggs floating across my eyes. Then I stood. I stood for minutes. I was afraid of sudden major dysfunction. The long scars throbbed. But I stood. Then

I fell back into the bed and slept. I did not dream.

Tellenbeck is upset. He has learned something. They do not want him back next year. He is a teacher. "Budget!" he says. He is very angry. "I'll tell you what it *is*," he says. "It is not their bleeding *budget*." He is pacing in my room. His glasses are crooked and his hair is mussed. His collar is unbuttoned and his tie is loose. He has been drinking alcohol. "They didn't like what I was saying about their precious Self-Antiself litany. They're jealous of my beautiful *machines*. That's what it *is*." His face is red and there are tears in his eyes. "Do you know what they call me behind my back?" I do not know. "They call me Mr. Fix-It. They call me Reddy Kilowatt. They call me the Thomas Edison of molecular biology!" I believe this means that they do not approve of Tellenbeck's machines. He takes a long drink of alcohol and coughs. "Jealous bastards," he says weakly. "Midgets."

We are sitting and watching Claude Rains. Tellenbeck has made snacks. It is embarrassing. He is trembling and his eyes are still wet. I would like to give comfort but I am not able to at this time. He takes a drink of the alcohol and pats my knee. He smiles sadly.

Claude Rains is wrapping himself in bandages. He can no longer see himself unless he does. There is a sadness in this. The village is unfriendly. There are many fear words. There is much unhappiness everywhere and there is anger.

I decide to stand. Right now, before his eyes. It will be a surprise. It will be a present. It will help his morale.

This time the polyester does not make the sickness come. I am stronger than before. "Look," I say. "Look!" I hold my arms out from my sides. My feet are together and my knees are locked. I am balanced. I think I am smiling. Tellenbeck spills his drink. He cannot believe it. It is weeks ahead of schedule. Thirty-nine days. It is marked on the calendar. And yet the fear of dysfunction is not strong in me. I am confident.

"Son of a bitch!" says Tellenbeck. He crawls over the bed toward me. He is intoxicated. He puts his arm around me and squeezes. I feel the air leave my lungs. I see the bright floating eggs. "My boy, my *boy!*" he says. He is having an emotion. I pat his shoulder. In this moment I feel that I might say his name or kiss his finger if he wishes.

"Kraft," I say, but my lips do not move.

"What was that? What did you say, Claude?"

I pat his shoulder. It is embarrassing. "Nothing," I say.

"I thought you said . . ."

I put my finger to his lips. He does not kiss. "Nothing," I repeat. "I said nothing."

The Sunbather approaches my chair. Tellenbeck has gone back to the apartment to get his cigarettes. "How is your mother?" the Sunbather asks. She is holding a thin book called *The River of the Higher Mind*. The name U. Eckstein is on the book in gold letters. "It's about the raised consciousness," she says. I am embarrassed. "I saw you looking at the title," she says, smiling. "Your lips were moving."

I remember to swallow. "My mother is . . ." I am having difficulty with the word.

"Oh, I'm so sorry," she says. She looks away.

I look away. I cannot swallow. I choke. "Dead," I say. It is a pain word. I cry. I am embarrassed but I cannot stop for the pain is deep and persistent. The Sunbather kneels by me and takes my hand. Her Tits are resting on my arm. They are warm and adhesive. They are big and heavy. I do not feel brittle.

"You've had a hard time of it, haven't you?" she asks. Her voice is agreeable. It rises and falls like music I have heard, and her breath is minted. She touches the scar at my wrist. She looks at my face and sees how it has been constructed. "Was it an automobile accident?" she asks.

"Yes," I answer, so quickly that I am surprised by it. It is a fib. It is not Someone Else's past. "I am recovering here with my uncle, Doctor Tellenbeck." It is a fib. "I am recovering here rather than at the hospital, for it is more pleasant." It is a fib. "I was hit by a truck in the fog," I say, fibbing. There is a new word I like very much. I use it now. "Smithereens," I say. "Smashed to Smithereens."

Tellenbeck returns. He sees the kneeling Sunbather and hesitates. He lights a cigarette and coughs a little.

The Sunbather looks up at him. "Your nephew has been telling me of his accident," she says.

Tellenbeck takes a large volume of smoke from his

cigarette and lets it come out slowly, on its own. He is squinting at me. "Has he?" he says.

Tellenbeck wheels me back into the apartment. "It is not time to go inside yet," I say. I am annoyed. "I was conversing with the Sunbather," I say. "I was telling her of my accident."

Tellenbeck undresses me and carries me to the bed. He attaches the inflatable sleeve to my arm and pumps it full of air. He watches the sphygmomanometer closely. "Low," he says. He lights another cigarette. He looks at me. "Your accident," he says. I look away. "What accident, Claude?" he asks.

It is embarrassing. "The truck in the fog," I say.

"Is that what you told the girl?" he asks. "That you were hit by a truck in the fog?" I nod my head without looking at him. "By God," he says. I still feel the heat of the Sunbather clinging to my arm. "By Jesus," says Tellenbeck.

We are riding. It is the first time. "This is called a freeway," says Tellenbeck. Our speed is sixty. I am seated next to him. I feel an imbalance when I look at the freeway sliding under the van. I look out the side window instead. There is a car next to us. It is moving at the same rate of speed. There is a Female driving. She is looking straight ahead and steering carefully. I do not see her Tits. I sit higher in my seat so that I can see her more fully. My eyes are nearly at the top of the window.

It is difficult. They are not visible. She is wearing a jacket made of heavy material. She looks at me. I am steaming the glass with my breath. She reduces the speed of her car and is swallowed up by the traffic behind us.

"See that ramp?" Tellenbeck asks. He is pointing to the right, across my face. "Remember it," he says. "It's called the Marbut Exit."

"Marbut Exit," I say, several times.

"That's where it happened," says Tellenbeck. "That's where the truck hit you in the fog." It is the fib plus another. Fib plus fib plus fib. I see an infinite series, the sum of which is me. "We might as well be consistent," says Tellenbeck. "As long as a cover story seems useful to us, it might as well be a good one."

"Smithereens," I say.

"Smithereens, nephew," says Tellenbeck.

We are riding next to The Green Sea. There is a chill that lies on my skin and begins to penetrate toward the bone. There is a dark barrier of fog hanging over the water several miles from the shore. There are many birds. The birds stand on the gray sand in long quiet lines as if they are waiting for something to emerge from the fog that will tell them where to fly.

It is seven steps from my bed to the door. It is eighteen steps from the door to the kitchen. It is nine steps from the kitchen to the enclosed patio. The enclosed patio is fourteen steps in length and ten steps in width.

It is sixty-seven steps from the patio gate to the swimming pool. It is one hundred and ninety-two steps around the swimming pool.

It is eight steps from one side of my bed to the other. It is four steps from the foot of my bed to the TV set. It is two steps from the bathtub to the toilet. It is always one step to the Fly.

And when I reach him, he is gone.

Constance Whaler is speaking to me. "I'm so happy you're up and around," she says. "You must be a fast healer." Constance Whaler is the Sunbather. Passing the mailboxes, I saw her name. Her apartment is 8–A. There are nine hundred and sixty-four steps around the condominium. I have taken six hundred and two. The condominium has a name. It is called The Sun Spot. From a distance it looks like weathered wooden boxes that have been placed in careless stacks on the top of a hill. Large windows the color of smoke all face west and in the late afternoon the sun is reflected back into The Green Sea one hundred and thirty times. The large windows look out across the water and the barrier of fog which is always there. Sometimes the fog comes close to the shore. Sometimes the fog moves toward the horizon until it is only a shining gray band in the distance. Sometimes as the sun descends it burns through it like a welding torch. It is pleasant.

I am still using the cane though I do not think it is necessary any longer. Constance Whaler touches my arm as she speaks. We are close to her door. "Come," she says. Her smile is white and healthy. "I'll fix us a pot of tea."

I am surprised. Her apartment is nothing like Tellenbeck's. There are colors. There are pictures. Pleasant objects hang from the walls or sit on shelves. There are soft pillows larger than tables. There are no tables. And there are no machines. The smells are agreeable. It is nice.

"Call me Connie," she says. She brings the tea. It is hot. She points to a pillow. I sit.

"Connie," I say. There is no pain. There is pleasure in the word.

"What is your name?" she asks.

"Claude Rains," I say.

Connie claps her hands and laughs. "Perfect," she says. "Just perfect."

I am glad. "Yes," I say. "It is."

"Take off your cap and those dark glasses, Claude," she says.

I do it.

"That's better."

My hair is growing well. For a while Tellenbeck believed that it might not grow vigorously. But it did. It started after the brittleness went away. It started when Tellenbeck began to take me out into the sunlight and fresh air. It is long now and it covers many scars. It is thick and black. I comb and brush it daily. It shines.

"You're a shy one, aren't you?" Connie asks. I raise

my cup to my lips. It is very hot but I drink. "It's a lovely quality," she says. "Rare." I feel heat in my face. It is not from the tea. "You are quite handsome, did you know that?" she asks.

"My face was designed for sensitivity, balance, and intellectual dignity, with a contrasting touch of ready, light-hearted humor," I say.

Connie laughs. I laugh. It is the first time. I do not know why I am laughing. Something in her laugh makes me laugh. I am laughing very hard. I am spilling my tea. My leg is burning but I cannot stop. It is enjoyable. There are tears in my eyes.

"You're a card to boot," says Connie. "Your liver must be beautiful."

I do not understand. My liver functions well. I am no longer afraid of major dysfunctions of the vital organs, but I do not think of them as beautiful.

"My mentor says that the liver is the seat of humor," Connie says. She touches herself under the rib cage. The Tits rise. The Tits are long as well as wide. They are heavy. I would like to see them without straps and fabric.

"Do you know what my mentor says about humor?" she asks.

I do not know. I am surprised that she thinks I should.

"He says it's the soul's ballast."

"U. Eckstein," I say, remembering her book, but watching her Tits.

"Right!" she says, and they jump. "*U* for Uranus, like the planet."

She is pleased with me. I am happy. I feel disturbances among my internal organs, an increase in the metabolic functions. My lungs require more air and there is perspiration. My hands, which were cold, are warm. My feet, which were warm, are cold. I am experiencing a sinking imbalance to the left. I am not frightened, though my heart is increasing its pulse. There is a large volume of saliva which I must swallow. I raise my cup and hope that she will not hear my throat cluck.

The time for my walk is over and I must leave. I do not want to go yet. But I do not want to make Tellenbeck worry. I stand. "Thank you," I say.

"We'll do it again," she says, taking my hand. "Soon."

My heart is moving large volumes of blood. I feel an imbalance, this time to the right and rising.

"Are you all right, Claude?" she asks. I touch my forehead. She holds my arm. I touch her hand. My head all at once is buried in her smell. There is a violent stick knocking at my thighs. It is not my cane. It is the external organ. It feels brittle as glass and is many times enlarged. It is a dysfunction. The first. I am frightened.

Tellenbeck is very interested. He takes off my clothes and has me lie down on the table. The dysfunctioning organ is very large and straining to increase its enlargement. It is painful. Perhaps it will rupture and hemorrhage. "Prepare the plasma, Doctor Tellenbeck," I say. My voice is shaky and rising uncontrollably.

Tellenbeck does not seem to notice my distress. "Champion," he says. It is an approval word. I am confused. "I didn't think Luigi would work. Didn't think we'd get off the ground with it," he says. He taps it with a pencil. "Champion," he says again. He is smiling. I see that he is pleased. It is confusing. There is a principle I do not understand.

"Is it not a dysfunction, then?" I ask.

He looks at me. He laughs. He pats me on the shoulder. "No," he says. "It is not a dysfunction, old scout."

I am happy to hear this. "The Luigi is normal?"

Tellenbeck laughs again. "Perhaps a cut above normal, Claude."

I look at this Luigi. It is esthetically displeasing. It is dark as a branch and unsymmetrical. It stands as if with a will of its own. It nods and jerks as if with rebellious fury. A curious notion enters my thoughts. This Luigi will create difficulties for me. That is the notion I have. This Luigi will become a troublemaker.

"Luigi is just a nickname, Claude," says Tellenbeck. "After the donor."

The word *donor* is not a pain word but it is one I do not like to hear. Tellenbeck speaks often of "the donors." I know that I am a composite of many donor parts. I know that Tellenbeck has made cellular compatibility

possible with his biotronic machines. But I do not wish
to hear of it. It is like the disturbing Fables. The Frog
Prince, The White Snake, and Sweetheart Roland. I
have torn these out of the book and destroyed them for
I do not want Tellenbeck to mention the titles acci-
dentally, even though I am sure he would not. I wish
now that I could forget them. When Tellenbeck speaks
of the donors, I remember the disturbing Fables against
my will. I have asked Tellenbeck to strap me to the
table and use the biodrill to scrub them out of my brain
but he says that is inadvisable since the memories are
mine and not Someone Else's and it would be foolhardy
to invite mnemonic dysfunction at this time. If *donor*
was a pain word he would not mention it in my presence
again. But it is not.

My Luigi awakens me from the dream. The giant
Female has taken me in her arms. The giant is grunting
close to the castle. The clock ticks. The giant Female is
frightened. Her scars are healing well. Except for a
crimson stripe here and there, they are invisible. My
hands are on her. I am pushing with unimagined
strength. "Rupture mc," she says. Then Luigi awakens
me. It is frightening at first and then I remember Tellenbeck's reassurances: "Not to worry, old son. You're a
big boy now."

I no longer use the cane. I no longer count my steps.

I walk as if I have always walked. There is great pleasure in this. Tellenbeck is amused. "You're swaggering, Claude," he says. I am only walking. First the left foot, then the right. Rise on the toes, flex the calves, bring down the heel. One two three four. One two three four.

I jog. I jog around The Sun Spot. Sometimes I jog all the way to the edge of The Green Sea. Fear of major dysfunction is distant in my memory. My hands are no longer cold. Every organ is in blossom. The blood beats in my wrists and neck. Boom boom. I enjoy touching the slow, even pulse. Tick tock.

I have gained forty pounds. I now weigh one hundred and fifty. It is increasing every day. I note the ounces. Tellenbeck no longer carries me into the workshop for my daily examination. I am too heavy and there is no need. He no longer carries me to the bath. He has returned the wheelchair to the rental firm. My hand is steady and capable of fine movement. I no longer color. I tie knots in rope instead. It is a form of art. The knotted ropes are intricate. They are pleasing to look at. I hang them on the walls of my room. My room is esthetically neutral. I have mentioned this to Tellenbeck. He appeared to be confused. He scratched his cheek and repeated my words to himself as if trying to sort out the meaning.

"What's wrong with your room?" he asked.

"Just look," I said.

He looked. He looked again. But he did not see. It is like the Fly. He looks but he does not see.

"It is a cipher," I said. "It is unappealing."

He shrugged his shoulders and lit a cigarette. "La de *da*," he said, and walked away.

So I hang my ropes with their pleasing knots on the vacant walls to make them attractive. Tellenbeck appears to admire what I have done. I do not really think he does. He feels it is his duty to patronize my small accomplishments. But I do not think he is pleased or displeased. He does not see. Often, when we are watching TV together, he will say, "So what's the big *deal?*" He uses this phrase to express his distaste for a commercial message or sometimes for the program itself. He did not say this when I showed him my hanging ropes. But the expression on his face was the same. Eyebrows raised, the nostrils dilated, the mouth tightened and turned down slightly at the corners. It means he is impatient and uninterested. It means he has better things to occupy his intelligence with. It means he thinks the hanging ropes are less interesting than the vacant walls. He does not see.

THE ATTACK was unprovoked. There was no purpose. I was jogging down the hill from The Sun Spot. I was preoccupied with a knot. The reverse double half-hitch, or the common lark's head. It is an important knot. I wish to learn all the important knots. I wish to excel. It is enjoyable to work out problems in my thoughts while I jog. The heart lifts large volumes of blood to my brain. My muscles swell.

I did not see the animal. It gave no warning. It crossed the grass quickly, a low growl humming in its jaws. It bit my ankle. I stopped. A Female came out of the house. "Oh!" she said. "Naughty boy!" She was elderly. If she intended to rebuke the animal, the animal did not respond. He tried to bite me again. She rebuked him again. Her rebukes seemed to encourage the animal. "He won't hurt you, young man," she said.

"He *has* hurt me," I said. It was not a large animal, but it was tubular and solid and its jaws were strong. Its eyes were yellow and bulging out of their sockets. I became frightened.

"Here, Leland," said the elderly Female. Leland did not obey. He succeeded in biting my leg again. "*Leland!*" said the Female. "Don't be a nuisance, you naughty pup!"

Leland, driven by the whining rebukes of the Female, began to leap. His sharp yelps hurt my ears. He was trying to bite me in a higher place. I saw my blood staining my new slacks. Tears came to my eyes. My lips were trembling.

"Leland, you are pestering the nice man!" said the Female.

Leland bit my hand. I saw that Leland had a loose band of red plastic around his neck. When Leland jumped at me again, I caught the plastic band and held it. I lifted Leland into the air. Leland whistled. Leland passed little claps of gas. His stubby legs sought traction in the air. They were unsuccessful. His eyes bulged farther out of their sockets. "Oh, please, *don't!*" said the elderly Female. She covered her opening-and-closing mouth with her fingers. "Leland is old!"

I said, "Old animals should not bite passing joggers." At first I did not release Leland because I was afraid to. I was afraid he might resume his unjustified attack. Then my motive changed. I did not release Leland because I enjoyed holding him aloft by the red plastic band. He had hurt me without reason. I did not provoke him. The Female had rebuked him. Yet he bit me. "Leland must be punished," I said. Leland had stopped whistling. His legs moved with less vigor. His eyes still bulged but now they looked sleepy and distant rather than enraged.

"I will punish him!" said the Female. "I promise you I will! Only please let him go!" Leland's legs were hanging limply in the air. Their delicate bone structure was touching. The little black claws. "Oh God, you're killing him!" she said.

I did not wish to kill. I lowered him to the grass. He began to whistle again. He got to his feet and ran to the arms of the waiting Female.

"Mother is going to restrict your toys until Friday, young man!" she said loudly.

"Do not be too severe," I said, and jogged to the beach.

We are in the zoo. It is part of my education. I have never seen animals in such numbers and varieties. It is very exciting. Tellenbeck tells me the natural history of each animal. I am interested but I am more interested in the animals themselves. The big cats sleep or pace. The dog-faced bears mock themselves for crackers. The monkeys intimidate one another. The tropical birds are exquisitely stupid. The gorillas are mysterious.

Of all the animals in the zoo, the gorillas are the only ones who see. The elephants are a possible exception, but it is difficult to be certain. Tellenbeck has finished his lecture on the territorial habits of the lowland gorilla but I do not wish to leave them yet. Jake, the eldest of the huge creatures, has fixed his glance on the spectators. There is something in his eyes that cannot be smiled at. The spectators laugh and taunt him but he is not affected by this as are the bears who will perform for crackers. This gorilla is looking at the thing that lies inside their excited chatter. He sees it.

One of the spectators crushes a sheet of paper into a ball and throws it across the moat. It bounces against the gorilla's massive head and falls to the ground at his feet. Jake picks the paper up. There is dignity in the movement which cannot be smiled at. His fingers are thick but they work carefully and with patience. I am sure he could tie complex knots if he could be persuaded it was a worthy pastime. He opens the crushed paper slowly. He smooths it out. He frowns at it and holds it close to his eyes. He appears to be searching for something. Perhaps a message. His scrutiny is careful and dignified. It is as if he is telling the spectator who threw it that he will give the paper thoughtful consideration for anything of value it might contain. He seems to be saying that if he finds anything of value there, he will treat it with the respect and honor it deserves. Jake is in no hurry. His movements are ponderous yet graceful. When he appears to have satisfied himself, he folds the paper carefully in half and daubs his anal sphincters with it. He wipes with daintiness. He wipes with affection, a look of rarefied contemplation on his leathery face. Then he crushes the paper into a ball again and in a movement swifter than the spectators believe possible, he hurls it back at the Person who threw it in the first place. The spectator tries to avoid the paper, but it strikes him on the shoulder. The spectator howls and barks like the nervous baboons. It is amusing.

I am remembering a gasping fish on white stones. A careful, long-legged bird, wading. There are tall trees around me and cold wind. There is a guitar weaving chords behind the trees. The sound of moving water fills my brain. It is Someone Else's past. Tellenbeck must be told.

I am in the sauna room of The Sun Spot. The heat is good. There are others here. There is talking and joking. I am increasing my strength with weight machines and barbells. I exercise for one hour and then I enter the sauna room. I am becoming strong. I am pleased with the growth and strength of my muscles. I can lift a weight over my head that exceeds the weight of my body, which is one hundred and eighty pounds. My skin is becoming tanned. I sit by the pool when the sun is high. My body takes heat from the sun like a sponge takes water. The sun fills me and increases me. The sun enters my muscles and nourishes them.

Two men are standing in front of me. I am on the third bench, where the heat is the greatest. The men are looking at me strangely. Their skin is white and splotched with pink. Their stomachs are large and their muscles are hidden beneath shimmering layers of fat. They are looking at my Luigi. "The goddamn hell," says one of the men.

"Where did you get that piece of artillery, fella?" asks the other.

I do not understand. I look where they are looking. The Luigi is dormant. "I do not know what you mean," I say. I look at their Luigis. I do not see them at first. And then I do. Gray acorns. And then I understand their questions.

"Where did you get that nasty *honk*, boy?" the man repeats.

"From Luigi," I say.

"Goddamndest thing I've ever seen," he says.

"A forking boxcar," says the other.

"More like a chunk of sewer pipe," says the first man.

"This Luigi a transplant surgeon, or something?"

I do not know who Luigi was. I do not know who

any of the donors were. It is an unpleasant subject. I bring my thighs together and conceal Luigi from their curious eyes.

I am remembering Sweetheart Roland against my will. The drops of blood are conversing with the hag. The subject of the donors always brings back a memory of the disturbing Fables. I am thinking of The White Snake. The mistreated servant of the King has learned the language of the animals. I do not wish to think of such things. I close my eyes and press my fists against my temples.

"Sorry, fella," says one of the men. "We didn't mean to get personal."

I no longer jog. It is because of Leland and others like Leland. Tellenbeck says, "We are not going to risk an infection. We are not going to let everything go down the tubes because of a crappy little mutt." Tellenbeck paces back and forth. He is home all the time now because he no longer teaches. They did not grant him tenure. "Budget!" he says, but Tellenbeck knows the truth. They believe his ideas are suspect. They have heard of his so-called biotrons. They ridicule him behind his back. "I lost Alpha Five to an earwig," he says. I wonder if Alpha Five ever felt the sun reach down into his muscles.

I am reading the TV schedule. "Look," I say. "*The Invisible Man* is on Classics of Yesteryear." Tellenbeck does not care. He looks at me and does not speak. He leaves the room and closes the door. He is depressed about his job. I understand. I hear him in the kitchen, opening cupboards. He is looking for the alcohol. I have hidden it again. Tellenbeck has begun to drink continuously. It is not good for his health. I hid his bottles behind the refrigerator this time. The refrigerator is heavy and it will be difficult for him to move it away from the wall.

Tellenbeck comes back into my room. "All right, Claude," he says. "Where did you hide it?" He is angry but he is forcing the anger out of his voice and face. But I see it in his shoulders. I see it in his arms. I see it in his neck. "*Where?*" he says. I am working on a chain of half-hitches. It requires my attention. "All right, laddy-buck," he says. "I'll go out for it, if that's what you want."

It is not what I want. I want him to stay home and make snacks and read the Fables to me after the Network Movie. I want him to drink tea or ginger ale. I want it to be the way it was before he lost his job. I want to say these things but I am not able to. I am embarrassed.

There is a meaningless syllable in my throat. It grows. It seeks form. My lips are trembling. My jaws spring apart. There is violence in them and the crude syllable explodes, over and over, tearing my throat, hurting my ears, bringing tears to my eyes. But Tellenbeck does not hear it. He is gone.

Marlene Steel is Connie Whaler's friend and Zip Porter is Marlene Steel's friend but I do not think that Connie Whaler is Zip Porter's friend. I do not know why I think this is so because Zip Porter is the friendliest Person I have ever seen. We are in Connie's apartment having tea. Zip Porter and Marlene Steel came in while Connie was telling me about *The River of the Higher Mind*. "Not the thinker who thinks he thinks," she said, "but the seer who simply sees." I did not understand. "Look," she said. "I'm talking about the *thinker* behind the thinker." I still did not understand. "Okay," she said, pointing to a large picture on the wall. It was a picture of yellow and red flowers. "What do you see?" she asked.

"Flowers," I said.

"*Who* is seeing the flowers?" she asked.

"I am," I said.

"That's an understandable response," she said. "But what I'm asking you, is, *who* is doing the *seeing?*"

It was very confusing. "Claude Rains," I said.

Connie clapped her hands together and laughed. "Perfect," she said. Then the doorbell rang and it was Marlene Steel and Zip Porter.

Zip Porter is wearing a blue suit and a red tie and does not want to sit on the floor. He puts two of the large pillows together and sits on them. When he looks up at us he is smiling. He has a fine smile. The smile is not just on his face. It is in his voice. When he speaks you can hear the words smiling. The smile is also in his shoulders and arms, it is in his hands and fingers.

He has long silver hair and glasses the color of lemonade. There are two diamonds on his right hand and a gold chain on his left wrist. Connie said, "I want you to meet my neighbor, Claude Rains."

Zip Porter held his hand out to me and I took it. There was no strength in his smiling fingers. "You mean *Claude* Rains the actor?" he asked, his smile growing larger and whiter.

"No," I said. "I am not the actor. Though I am named after him."

Zip Porter took his hand away and looked at it. "Terrif," he said.

I am remembering a similar occasion. It is larger. It is filled with excitement. There are more people than anyone had expected and there is to be an important series of introductions upon which many valued things will depend though everyone present is attempting to minimize the significance of the event. Several people, however, are openly nervous. They are chattering in each other's faces. A large man, openly disdainful, is tapping his foot and eating a bird. Tellenbeck must be told.

Marlene Steel is telling Connie about something very crucial to her future. "Zip has agreed," she says, "to let me have a show in the mall!" It is good news. Connie takes Marlene in her arms and hugs her.

"Hey," says Zip Porter. He is picking between his

front teeth with a silver nail. "How about me? Don't I get one?"

Connie gets up and goes to him but there is a stiffness in her walk that is unnatural to her. She touches Zip on the shoulder and presses her cheek on his.

"Mildo," says Zip. "Luke warmo. Coolish. Tepid." These are words of criticism but his smile is friendlier than before.

Connie becomes embarrassed. Her cheeks redden under the tan. "I'll get us more tea," she says.

"Tell me what you do," says Zip. He is speaking to me.

"Do?" I ask. Zip looks at Marlene and winks.

I look at Marlene. She is pretty. Her hair is long and black. She is wearing a man's shirt and denim slacks. There are spots of paint on the shirt. I am looking for the outline of her Tits. But the shirt is too loose. I think they are small. She is smoking a brown cigarette.

"I bet he's the local physical therapist," she says. She is smiling now and watching my eyes. It is embarrassing.

"How about it, Mr. Rains?" says Zip. "You the local P.T. man?" I do not understand. "How about those muscles, Marl?" he says.

"Hubba, hubba, hubba," she says, moving around on her pillow. The movement draws the loose shirt tight and I see the outline of her Tits, which are small, just as I thought, but high and pointed unlike Connie's which slope down heavily and taper.

"When did you make the big switch from mystics to

jockoes, Con?" says Zip when Connie comes back with the tea. There is something elusive in the conversation. I am trying to grasp it.

"Claude is my *neighbor*," Connie says. "And he is *not* an athlete."

Marlene raises her eyebrows and blows smoke into the air. "All that meets the eye," she says musically.

"Hey, abba *dabba*," says Zip, shaking the smiling fingers of his right hand.

We are in 14–D on the fourth floor of The Sun Spot. It is vacant and available. Marlene Steel is going to take it. The manager has given Connie the key. Zip is opening the closets and looking inside. "Let's see," says Marlene, pressing her finger against her cheek. "Let me get my bearings." She is standing near the large window that overlooks The Green Sea. "I think this will have to be the studio. This is where the light is." The sun is entering the barrier of fog. Where it touches the fog, there is a pool of light. The sun becomes flat and ragged, crimson and weak. It is a touching moment. I enjoy sunsets.

"Look," I say to the others. They join me at the window.

Connie touches my hand. "Magnificent," she says.

"Listen," says Zip. "I expect to see a gaggle of *Sunsets at Sea* in the show, Marl."

Marlene covers her mouth with her hands. "Retch, retch," she says.

"Beauty is so unpopular these days," says Zip. "You'd

think a sunset at sea was an inferior spiritual experience to looking up a chicken's ass, to hear these artistos talk about it." These are words of criticism, but the friendliness of his smile is not diminished. It occurs to me that Zip Porter must be a wonderful Person to have critical thoughts and yet remain undisturbed by them. "How about you, Claudio?" he says. "Do you prefer a chicken's ass to a sunset at sea?"

I have never seen a chicken's ass. Tellenbeck has brought me many books. I have learned very much. I can name presidents and vice-presidents, kings and queens, wars, insurrections, and mutinies. I am very good in mathematics. I am up to G in the Oxford dictionary. One of my books is *Ornithology for the Millions*. I am trying to remember the part about domesticated birds.

"The chicken's anal region," I say, "is covered with a fine down."

Connie laughs. Marlene laughs, too. Marlene stands next to me and touches my bicep. "Oh my," she says, and presses her fingernails against the skin.

I feel a chill. Her black hair is very close to my face. I smell it. Luigi rolls over and thumps awake. "I must go, now," I say quickly. "My uncle will worry."

Marlene catches my hand. "Now that we're neighbors, you'll have to come up sometime for tea." She is squeezing my hand. Luigi is flogging his confines.

I have to swallow and I am sure that she hears my throat clucking. "Yes," I say, pulling my hand from hers. "I will." I turn my back quickly and leave.

"Check you later, stud," says Zip.

Tellenbeck will not read. I have left the book open to the Fable I want but he ignores it. He is drinking. He now hides the bottles from me so that I cannot hide them from him. He is pretending to drink ginger ale but I can smell the alcohol. It is a bad smell. I pick up the book and read the Fable to myself, aloud.

This place under the false sky is called The Center. It is a large complex of joined buildings. All the buildings are under one roof. Simulated daylight is radiated from the ceiling from invisible sources. There are many shoppers and strollers. There are many simulated plants and trees. There is music. It seems to come from an infinite distance, though it is very clear.

"You can get anything you want here," says Connie. "Stereos, cars, furniture, groceries, office machines, patio covers, fireplaces, stamp collections, toys, imported cigars. You name it."

We go into a small store. There are books on all the walls and many more on tables. Connie goes to an area that is designated as "Occult." She picks up a book called *Thee, the Tree*. It is by Uranus Eckstein. She turns the first few pages. "Mind and tree are locked in the eternal embrace," she reads. "But where is the eye that sees this?" Connie looks at me and smiles. I know that she does not expect me to reply. But I shrug anyway.

We go back out onto the mall. There are benches and

fountains. Lights at the base of the fountains throw rainbows of color into the rising water. It is beautiful.

Marlene Steel is waving at us. She is dressed in a long
white robe with beads stitched into the fabric. She has
several silver bracelets on each arm. She is having her
show. There are a dozen or more paintings on display.
Four of the paintings are sunsets at sea, but they are in
error because there is no fog, near or far. The horizon is
a blue line that divides sea and sky. Even so, they are
attractive.

Zip Porter joins us. He is the manager of The Center.
He is still friendly but appears to have little time for
conversation. He looks at his watch often as he speaks
and finally says, "Check you later."

Marlene opens her purse and shows us her money. It
looks like a small head of lettuce. "Sunset money,
friends," she says. "Lunch is on me."

We go into a place called The Tangent. It is dark, but
the ceiling is lit with neon tubes in the shape of geo-
metric figures. Triangles, parallelograms, circles, rhom-
buses, and other polygons. We take a booth under a pale
blue isosceles triangle. A Female with large, pink Tits
brings us water. They are powdered. They are creamy.
"Suck your eyes back in your head, Claude," says Marlene. I breathe saliva and choke. I hold the large menu in
front of me. "The poached salmon," says Marlene.

"The same," says Connie.

I do not understand the menu. I finally manage to
swallow. "Poached salmon," I say.

Zip Porter joins us. He looks at his watch and sits down next to Marlene. "What are we having, troops?" he asks.

"The fish," says Marlene.

"Hey, retch retch!" he says. He signals for the waitress. I do not watch her approach. But out of the corner of my eye, I see undulating pink. "Listen, I'll have that Veal Prince Orloff," he says, "with a side of cheese ravioli."

The Riesling contains alcohol. I did not know that. It did not smell like the alcohol that Tellenbeck drinks. I believed it to be a type of ginger ale. Less sweet and without bubbles. Less good. But I drank a glass and then another.

Marlene is counting her money. "Fifteen percent of that belongs to the house," says Zip.

"Two hundred and eighty-five," says Marlene, returning the bills to her purse. "Five sunsets at sea and three transcendent gulls," she says.

"Well, it's well known that the public wants beauty. The public wants pictures that boost the old morale," says Zip.

"The public would eat horse apples if they came out heart-shaped," says Marlene.

"No, hey, listen. I'm serious," says Zip.

"We know you are," says Marlene.

I feel good. These are my friends. I am warm. The Riesling has warmed the surface of my skin. My face is radiating warmth. I think of my face as a small sun, giving warmth to my good friends at this table. I pour myself a third glass of Riesling.

"Hey, abba dabba," says Zip.

"Abba dabba," I say, raising my glass. I am smiling and my friends are smiling. It is wonderful to be alive! "I do not feel at all like a monster," I say.

"That's what they invented vino for, Claude," says Zip.

"Were you feeling poorly, Claude?" asks Connie.

"No," I say. "I was feeling fine. But now I feel even better."

I stand on the seat. My thoughts are rapid and confused. I am having a strong memory of Someone Else's past. There is a room full of children. They are cheering and clapping their hands. Their parents are standing in the back of the room, in the shadows. The parents are applauding too, but I cannot see their hands.

"Hey, fellow, *fellow*," says Zip. It is odd. I see him, and the children, and the children's parents. And now, from somewhere, a spotlight is turned on. The children are cheering for the man who is throwing objects into the air. The man does not allow any of the objects to fall. Yet he keeps throwing them into the air. Tellenbeck must be told.

"For Pete's sake, Claude," says Zip. "Get *down*. You're doing a weird thing, Claude."

I am climbing up on the back of the seat. My head bumps a flickering octagon. Many people in The Tangent are looking at me. "And now, ladies and gentlemen,"

I say, "I will show you what a finger can do." I show them a rigid forefinger. I do not know what I am talking about or doing. "The famous Carlos Abrigán finger stand!" I say. Several men at the bar applaud. Zip has lost his smile. He is looking into his napkin, as if it might be there.

"Hold on a sec," says Marlene. "Let me get my bearings. What exactly is happening here?"

"Do not worry," I say. I show her my finger. "I have performed this many times. Barcelona. Madrid." I place my hands on the hard vinyl and swing my feet over my head. I am surprised that I am not surprised that I can do this. My feet are among the geometrical lights. I am careful not to break any. I shift my weight to my right arm and raise the left outward so that it is parallel to the table. My right hand is very powerful. Power surges into it from my nerves and arteries. It is surprising and rewarding. I am enjoying this immensely. Slowly I extend the fingers of my right hand. All my weight now rests on the tips of my fingers. Then, one by one, beginning with the thumb, I bring the fingers back into my palm until only the forefinger remains extended. My forefinger feels like a cylinder of hard wood, capable of bearing my entire weight for an indefinite period. All the men at the bar are applauding. Soon, everyone in The Tangent is applauding. I am very pleased. I like the sound of many hands clapping. It is a pleasure sound. I stay on my finger until the clappers grow weary.

Connie is sitting on the floor and looking out on The Green Sea. Her face is without expression and her eyes are focused on the horizon. Marlene is painting a picture. I am the model. She asked me to take my clothes off. I could not. She said, "Don't be backward, Claude. Think of me as your uncle, the doctor. Think of your body as anatomy."

I do think of my body as anatomy. I think of my anatomy all the time. I know that Marlene is a professional artist. But I cannot take off my clothes for her. Most of the scars are no longer visible, but I am not able at this time to stand before her unclothed.

I am looking out on The Green Sea as she paints. The fog is moving in from the horizon. There is a point of light centered in the fog. It is pale and green. It was dim at first. Then it grew brighter. Then the fog closed in and it disappeared.

Connie stands and stretches. "Ataraxia," she says. I do not remember the word. There is no pain. I look at Marlene.

"Blissout," she explains.

I look at Connie. "Without pills," she says, smiling.

I am driving the van. I like this holding the wheel and touching the pedals. I like this turning and signaling and this speed. The freeway as it slides under the van no longer creates an imbalance. Tellenbeck is watching me closely. He has placed the inflatable sleeve on my arm.

He pumps it full of air every few minutes and watches the sphygmomanometer. It is a test of my capacity to endure certain varieties of cultural pressure. "One-twenty over eighty-five," says Tellenbeck. I smile. I know that is good. "Don't get cocky, Claude," he says. The speedometer says sixty-five.

There are tall white towers of concrete and glass. I am reminded of the enchanted castle behind the briar rose. There are low flat black windowless structures with numbers on them. There are many people.

"State Polytechnic University," says Tellenbeck. "I wanted you to see it, Claude. In a way, it's the center of your universe, your source." We are driving along a narrow street that passes through the buildings of the University. "Oh brother," says Tellenbeck. "How I'd like to bring you up to Applied and have you strut in front of Caulkins, Schroeder, Yost, Hickerson, Isozu, Parkhurst, and Ungaretti!"

The thought of doing this frightens me. My foot touches the brake and we are jerked forward in our seats.

"Don't worry, Claude," Tellenbeck says. "I can't do it. I broke too many of their sacred rules. I cleaned out the meat safe. I swiped gear from all over campus. I falsified reports. I bribed a couple of lab assistants. I invented names to put on requisition slips. I ran disguised programs on the computers."

I am relieved.

"Still," he says, "great deeds have often required petty crimes."

I touch the brake again.

Tellenbeck laughs. He pats me on the shoulder. "No sweat, keed. I won't let them get at you. This world doesn't deserve my discoveries. Let them klutz their way back into the Dark Ages. Let them beat the same old bushes until the cows come home. It's no skin off my ass."

We are in the country. The speedometer is on forty. I am having a pleasing memory of busy wives. The wives have come in from the field. There is gossip and laughing. One is angry with another, but it is not serious. They all have knives. They are working at a table. The table is filled with fresh vegetables and a large unidentifiable carcass. Bread is baking. Smell the oven.

The road we are on is narrow and it rises into the hills. Beyond the hills are the Fish Mountains. Beyond the Fish Mountains lies the Great Desert. I have studied the map. The first town that you come to after the mountains is called Solar Flats. The average temperature there is seventy-nine degrees. The average rainfall is negligible.

I do not tell Tellenbeck of the memory of wives.

We are watching *The Invisible Man*. Tellenbeck is drinking again. I could take the bottle away from him by force now but it is unthinkable.

"What do you see in this dumb movie?" Tellenbeck asks. The question does not deserve intelligent comment. Claude Rains is wrapping himself in bandages. He can no longer see himself unless he does. The village is angry. There is much unhappiness in the countryside. Trouble is on the way.

I awoke in the kitchen. It was dark. I was standing in the middle of the room. I bumped the table, a dish crashed to the floor, and I awoke. Tellenbeck came in. He turned on the lights. "What gives?" he asked. "What's going on, Claude?" I did not know myself. It was confusing. I was naked. I covered myself with a dish towel. I looked at Tellenbeck. His face was tired and creased with strain. His eyes were red and the flesh around them was swollen. The short whiskers of his beard were gray. His hair was gray too. This surprised me so much that I forgot my own predicament for the moment.

"Jesus," he said. "Somnambulism."

I did not know the word.

"You've been sleepwalking, Claude," he said.

"Is it a dysfunction?" I asked.

"A minor one, perhaps," he said.

And then the feeling that everything that is happening now has happened before came over me. I became alarmed. Tellenbeck looked closely at my face. My teeth were chattering.

Tellenbeck put his hand on my arm. "Cool it, Claude," he said. "You're all right." I did not believe him. He went to the refrigerator and took out a bottle of yellow pills. "Swallow a couple," he said. I did. Soon, the feeling passed.

We sat down together at the kitchen table. Tellenbeck fried up some bacon. "Somnam-bulism," I said.

"Not to worry, Claude," said Tellenbeck. But I did.

Tellenbeck wears a hairpiece.

Connie is reading aloud from *Thee, the Tree*. Marlene is making a contour drawing of my latissimus dorsi.

"Love," says Connie, "can only be known by its effects."

Zip claps. He is lying on the floor and looking up at the ceiling. "Remember the mambo?" he asks. No one answers him.

"Just as light can only be defined by its *effects*," says Connie.

"Don't breathe for a sec," says Marlene.

"No one can say just what light *is*," says Connie. "Because its essence is unknowable. Its *effects*, however, are understood by all."

Zip claps. "Cha cha cha," he says.

"Or the Bunny Hop," says Zip.

"Okay, breathe, Claude," says Marlene.

"Toodle," says Zip, getting up. "Places to go, people to see."

Marlene sees him to the door. He touches her buttock and squeezes. She puts her finger in his ear. He kisses the air in front of her.

I quickly pull on my shirt. Marlene watches me. Her

eyes pierce. It is as if they have a biotronic probe in them. I look away. Though I no longer fear major dysfunction, I am always concerned with cellular integrity. That is why my watch does not have a radium dial. Tellenbeck says there is already too much junk radiation in the air now, no point in adding to it unnecessarily.

Connie is sitting on the floor with her legs crossed and looking out on The Green Sea at a thing in the distance. The sun glares off the water's surface. There are several boats with white sails. The boats rise and fall pleasantly in the undulating water. The fog is thin, a glossy line on the horizon. It does not look like fog. But it is fog. It looks like a river of running silver forty miles away. But it is fog.

Connie appears to be sleeping with her eyes open.

"She's merging," says Marlene.

"Is it like sleep?" I ask.

"According to Con, it's more like being away."

I do not understand. "Does she hear us?" I ask.

"According to Con, she hears more than we are saying." Marlene takes my hand and we step to one side of Connie's vision. "Am I right, Con?" Marlene asks. Connie does not look away from the distant thing, but her expression changes slightly.

Marlene pulls me away. She shows me the drawing of my back. It is embarrassing. The size of the muscles is exaggerated. She steps close to me and her small, high, pointed Tits scrape against my arm, raising bumps. Luigi lurches. I step away and turn to a painting of a tree. The tree is splintered. Smithereens. The sky is stormy and webbed with electricity. I concentrate on the painting. It is gray, brown, purple and black. There is a yellow bird on a branch, preening itself.

"What are you saving yourself for, Claude?" Marlene asks. "The Olympics?"

She pulls me into her bedroom. She removes her clothes in swift easy motions. I am unable to find a painting to study. I am unable to turn my eyes away. Her Tits are shaped in the way I imagined them. Cones.

"Fuck me," she says.

There is no pain in the unfamiliar word. I am well past the *F*'s in the large Oxford dictionary, but I do not remember this word.

"Don't tell me you *don't*," she says.

"Don't?" I repeat. It is a puzzle. There is something in the conversation that eludes my grasp.

"*Fuck*," she says. "F.U.C.K." I spell the new word aloud too.

"What does it mean?" I ask. Marlene falls on the bed and brings her knees up against her stomach. She is laughing. "Too much," she says. "Too *much*, Claude." She believes we are sharing a joke. I try to laugh a little, but it is not laughter. "Full, unlawful, carnal knowledge," she says slowly. "The whole treat, Claude."

She leaves the bed and embraces me. "Sweet, sweet dumbbell," she says. "Sweet Claude."

Her smell is strong. My breath lifts strands of her black hair. I am perspiring. There are disruptions of my internal organs. Luigi is shoving. There is a slow kettle-drum in my ear. The floor is not level. The giant has entered the building and the floors are tilting. I try to leave, but Marlene blocks the way out. A vision of explosive dysfunction makes me tremble. *Boom, boom, boom,* as each step he takes shakes the castle to its foundation. The magic goose has lost control and is releasing all its eggs. The giant Female has slipped into the closet. Marlene is doing something with her hands and I am too disturbed to stop her. "*Naarr,*" I say. I do not know where the syllable came from. "*Naaarrr.*" It makes me wince.

She looks at me and then at Luigi. She looks at Luigi and then at me. Her eyes are very wide and her mouth falls open. "What the Christ is *that?*" she asks.

"Luigi," I say.

She is covered with chillbumps and her nipples are like little turrets. I step toward her.

"No, wait a sec," she says. "Let me get my bearings."

"The whole treat," I say, not sure of the precise meaning of my words.

I SHOW Tellenbeck the painting. It is my tenth. Marlene is teaching me how to do it. "You're a fast learner, sweet," she said. And it is true. I am.

It is a picture of boats on The Green Sea with gulls circling the chum. Tellenbeck holds the canvas by the wooden frame and looks at it with his eyebrows raised. "Well, well," he says. Then he puts it down and goes into the workshop. I hear a machine humming. I am disappointed. Tellenbeck is indecipherable. He has been this way for some time. Still, I am disappointed. The painting is praiseworthy and I enjoy praise and he is wrong to withhold it.

I get the hammer and nails and hang the painting in the living room. Tellenbeck comes back. "What the be-jesus do you think you're doing, hotshot?" he asks.

"Hanging my picture," I say. "It will cheer up this room a bit."

Tellenbeck takes the picture down. "It isn't dry yet, Claude," he says. "It's smelling the place up. Besides, I don't like pictures hanging on the walls. I like blank walls. Easier to think clearly with blank walls." He goes back into the workshop. I take the painting into my room and hang it there, between the ropes.

I am very excited with these oils. They are more exciting than the binomial theorem or the trigonometric functions, which I have just learned. I can look at the shadow of a pyramid and tell its altitude without having to climb it, and that is fine, but this is different. This is finer. The pictures come out of my own hand. It is a mystery. It is like the memories which belong to Someone Else, except I know that the pictures are *mine*. They are gifts from my hand given to my eye. A closed circuit, a private cycle, and no one else is responsible for it. And each picture is a surprise. I am amazed that I possess such craft. Such design. Such sense of light and shade. Such color. I tremble at times with the strangeness of it. Marlene says I am a diamond in the rough. I understand what she means. Connie is excited too. Zip Porter says "abba dabba" or "zotz" whenever he sees my work. When my work is praised I feel my systole pressure ride into the two hundreds. I sometimes think my blood vessels will burst with pleasure. And I do not care!

The Network Movie is about a deranged painter who mutilates himself out of the intensity of his vision and the anguish he feels because of the need for praise which is not forthcoming and will not be forthcoming though it is clearly deserved. It is a wonderful movie. I cry.

"What a load of hooey," says Tellenbeck. "If there's anything that makes me puke it's morbid self-indulgence." He does not notice my tears, or if he does, he does not care to make comment at this time.

He has not made snacks tonight. There is no ginger ale in the refrigerator and there is no fresh endive. "The wolf is at the door," says Tellenbeck. He says it every night. The only money he receives now is an unemployment check and soon these will stop. It is depressing for him. I feel guilty and dishonorable for not feeling depressed too. But I am so pleased with my progress with the oils that I cannot share his gloom. There is no room in my thoughts for it. I am a diamond in the rough and happy.

I have not seen the Fly since he crawled into the air conditioner. I approached within two steps. He became alert. He stopped scrubbing his filthy legs and grooming his veinous wings. He knew I had reached the one-step barrier. "Bastardino," I whispered. *Bastardino* is a word that Zip Porter uses when in a critical frame of mind. I like it. "That bastardino," said Zip, "wouldn't know a good deal if it grew hair on its boffo and whistled 'Melancholy Baby.'" Zip was referring to a merchandiser who wanted to rent space in The Center but thought the fee was too high and the lease too constraining. "Nasty bastardino," I said. The Fly heard me. His honeycomb eyes glittered with an ugly incandescence. I had a can of poison spray in my hand. I slowly brought it from behind my back. Then, as his legs prepared to catapult the fat metallic body to safety, I pressed the button. The toxins engulfed him. A syllable of delight rose in my throat. The Fly, soaked in poison, staggered clumsily into the grille. Where he died. *Died.*

Someone in the exercise room played a joke on me. "Is that two hundred?" I asked.

"Two hundred even, Tarz," they said.

I gripped the bar and lifted. It was heavier than I remembered. I heard fabric tear. *I must be getting weaker,* I thought. The thought of a retrogression frightened me. Tellenbeck has mentioned the slight possibility of diapause: the upswing of the pendulum reaching its highest point, then the fall, the decay. And so, I exerted myself. I brought the bar up to my chest. My breath whistled through my teeth and there was a pounding in my brain. *The blood vessels,* I thought.

"I cannot do it," I said, the words strangled and hoarse. The men were laughing. I did not like their faces when they laughed.

"Give it hell, Bomba," someone said.

Bright blue eggs began to float before my eyes. The thought of deep visceral rupture and hemorrhage made me sag. And yet I could not lower the bar and admit that a retrogression had set in. I bent my knees slightly and heaved my arms upward. The bar moved. And then I locked my elbows and straightened my knees.

"Holy hernia," said one of the men. They were no longer laughing. They were touching each other on the shoulders and looking at the door. I lowered the bar to the floor. I counted the weights. An extra twenty-five-pound disc had been added to each end of the bar. I had pressed two hundred and fifty pounds. I was very pleased with the accomplishment. And then I was very disturbed.

"I could have hurt myself severely," I said to the men. I began to cry. I stepped toward them. They left the weight room quickly. "Bastardinos," I shouted after them.

Tellenbeck is angry. "Where the blue blazes have you been?" he asks.

"To Solar Flats," I say. "With Connie Whaler."

Tellenbeck is upset with me. He is making an electro-encephalogram. He is listening to my lungs. He is tapping my chest. He is looking between my toes. "Two days," he says. "Two *days*, Claude. What were you thinking of? Didn't you think I'd be out of my mind with worry?"

I do not know what to say.

"I've been far, far too lax with you, buster," he says. "I have only myself to blame, I suppose. I should have never allowed you so much freedom. I should have known you'd abuse it some day."

"Abuse freedom?" I ask. "I do not understand, Doctor."

"Don't you?" he says.

"No, I do not," I say.

Tellenbeck pulls a stool next to the table and sits on it. "Look, Claude," he says. His voice is unsteady. His mouth is unstable at the corners. I believe he is trying to control an emotion. "What you do, where you go, is *my* responsibility," he says. "I set the limits, Claude. I've never come right out and said it in so many words, but I thought you were intelligent enough to understand that. Are you testing my authority?" Such thoughts have never occurred to me. Freedom, limits, abuse, authority. I owe Tellenbeck everything. He is a genius. Where would I be today if it were not for him? "What if I told you that you will no longer be allowed to see these new friends of yours?" he asks.

The thought is painful. It is the first time a thought has caused pain. It is not as severe as the pain from a pain word, and it does not affect the cerebral hemisphere directly, but it brings the tears more quickly to my eyes.

Tellenbeck is looking at the moving graph. "Hey, that put a rill or two in those valleys," he says. "Generally speaking, though, your alpha is improving. Background noise down, fewer high-velocity spindles. The crests are pancaking slightly. There's more yeast in those troughs."

I take the device from my head and sit up. "You would not do that, would you Doctor Tellenbeck?" I ask.

"Do what?" he asks. He is making a notation on his clipboard.

"Forbid me to see my friends again?" I slide off the table. Tellenbeck is half my size. He seems frail. Brittle. I look down on him.

"It might be necessary, Claude," he says, not looking up from his clipboard. He hears the noise in my throat. He looks up at me, his glasses down on his nose. He looks bewildered for a moment.

"No," I say. "It will not be necessary." He is backing away from me. He is frightened. I will not harm him. I do not harm. I am sweet. Marlene Steel says so. She is right. I am.

"You have to obey me, Claude," he says. "You depend on me." It is a fib.

"For what?" I ask. He will have to invent another fib.

Because I do *not* depend on him.

"Listen," he says, bumping into a cabinet. "You're a goddamned *zoo*. Everything seems to be going all right now, but it's only been months, Claude. Anything can happen. In fact, I'm expecting a diapause any day now. Look, I've been preparing drugs to combat it." He holds up some test tubes.

The word *diapause* frightens me. It is a fear word. It means growth stops. The harmony of growing cells will stop, wobble, and reverse. It means the setting in of a retrogression.

"Each part, from each donor," says Tellenbeck, "might trigger a massive, cell-mediated rejection. Civil war, Claude. You'd turn into a bleeding prune in ten minutes."

I faint.

Tellenbeck is slapping my wrists and putting water to my lips. "Claude, *Claude*," he says. "The chances are a thousand to one against, Claude. I was just trying to scare a little sense into you."

I do not answer him. I push the water aside. I go to my room and put on my sweat suit.

"Come off it, Claude," says Tellenbeck. "Don't be a sorehead."

I do not answer. I go to the weight room and press two hundred and sixty pounds three times, easily.

Connie said: "I'd like you to meet him, Claude. You'd like him." The idea of driving to Solar Flats and meeting a new Person who might be another friend was pleasing to me. Then I would have four. I cannot include Tellenbeck. I could say *five* if I included him. I would like to say *five* but I am not able to at this time and perhaps I may never be able to for Tellenbeck is changing and closeness was difficult even in the beginning when I depended on him for everything. Besides, there are many others. There are Persons everywhere. Sometimes when my eyes meet the eyes of a stranger I feel a joining. It is very exciting. Words are not required. Words are the final bonding if the words are warm and sincere. There are many possible bondings. I see an infinite series of bondings. Five, Six, Seven, Eight, Nine, Ten . . . $N-1$, N. N friends! And $N+1$, $N+2$, and so on, forever. It is wonderful. I am very happy.

The desert is hot and clear. Solar Flats shimmers in the warping air. It is a small town of old houses, garages, and cafés. Connie pulls the car up to a café called Bully's.

"This is it," she says.

"This is where he works?" I ask.

"This is where he *lives*," she says.

We enter. It is very small. There are no customers. We sit at the counter. A fat man is standing at the stove with his back to us. He is cleaning the grill with a flat stone and humming.

"Hi, Bully," says Connie in a loud voice.

The fat man turns. His face is round and blank as a dish. Then it changes. "Connie Whaler!" he says. It is a roar. His face is splitting. His eyes are almost swallowed in fat when he smiles. His teeth are brown and there is a gray stubble on his chin. He is not handsome. "Hey," he says, making his face serious and stern, the eyes reemerging from the fat. "You haven't been to see me in more than, what, a *year*, little girl!"

Connie takes his hand. They kiss. I am embarrassed. I feel outside. I see the joining of their friendship and in this moment I am joined to no one. I look at the walls. There is a large photograph of a white mountain. "Visit the Alps," it says. Two large fans hang from the ceiling. They turn slowly. There are many small flies. I am uneasy.

"This is Claude," says Connie when the fat man releases her. I take his hand. He has Tits. "I want you to meet my mentor, Claude. Uranus Eckstein."

I am surprised. I did not expect a fat cook. I do not know what I expected. But I did not expect to meet Uranus Eckstein in a small café like this cleaning a grill with a flat stone.

"The Uranus tag is just for book sales," he says. "Call me Bully. It's a version of Burleigh. But don't call me Burleigh." He picks up a cleaver and chops an onion in half. "You can't sell books on mysticism in this neck of the woods unless your name has the right ring to it. Now, 'Uranus' *sells*." He laughs. His laugh is large. Connie laughs. And then I laugh, too. There is a joining. Bully cooks us three cheeseburgers and we eat them with tall Cokes on ice.

We are sitting in Bully's back yard on a large bench-swing, drinking iced Coke. It is evening and the desert is cooling quickly.

"That desert," says Bully. "Isn't it something? The tail end of the world."

Connie is sitting between us. We are rocking the bench-swing back and forth slightly. The desert lies before us flat and brown, like a sea without tides. It is pleasant.

"I love it," says Bully. "Only the moon, The Sea of Tranquillity, could possibly beat it."

At the end of the flat part of the desert, just above a low range of black mountains, the full moon rises. It is orange and bloated. The color of the moon reminds me of a Fable, *The King of the Golden Mountain,* which pleases me very much. I am reminded of the King's flask filled with the Water of Life. I drink the cold Coke and refill my glass from the quart bottle before us. The dry air has made me thirsty.

"I used to hate it," says Bully. "I'd drive through it like a man waltzing over hot coals in his socks. One thought in my head: get your rosy cheeks to the other side of this place, pronto!"

Connie has a small notebook open on her lap. She is writing in it.

Bully leans forward suddenly and looks at me. "You ever been in sales promotion, Claude?" he asks.

"No," I say, although I do not know what sales promotion is.

"Let me tell you a little story," he says.

"I enjoy stories very much, Bully," I say.

"Then you probably understand something about D.D.T.," he says.

"D.D.T.?" I ask.

"Dread, Despair, and Terror," he says. "All good stories are laced with it in one way or another," he says. "And that's because the world is riddled with it, inside and out, armpit to armpit, just like bugspray." Bully pauses to drain his glass and belch three times. "Just like love," he says, "you know D.D.T. through its effects. That's why stories are so good at telling you *what* it is without trying to nail it down. All the big guns in the mysticism game use the parable, Claude. Philosophers have tried to reduce the truth of parables to something you can fiddle with in the lab, but those dildos have been stirring up the hive for a number of years now and I've yet to see any *honey*." He pats Connie on the knee and belches again. "Hey, you getting this, Con?" he asks. "I feel like a worm on a hot rock. I'm jumping, Con."

"Picture Vegas, '56 or '57," says Bully. "Got it? Okay."

I know there is such a place. I have seen photographs.

"Picture two hundred ambitious young hotdog dildos in gray suits and knit ties and little buttons on their lapels that say *Get It While It's Hot!* Picture their wives, all with the same corsage and little pillbox hat. We've taken over this hotel. It's been a hectic few days, setting up the organizational details. Picture a mini-convention. Oceans of good booze, some incautious gambling, floor shows with a hundred gals dressed in ostrich feathers. Lobster tail and filet mignon every night. Denver omelets and Bloody Marys every morning. The pace is terrific. Bip bip bip. Some dildo always shoving a drink at you, a paper cup full of Oysters Rockefeller, a revised schedule. Hustlers on the hustle. A platoon of comers showing each other their stuff. Picture it, Claude.

"I was giving my speech. We were in the hotel's convention center. 'In ten years,' I said, 'No! In *five* years, The Bully Burger will be a household word!' That did it. They stood up in their chairs. They clapped, stamped and yodeled. They kissed each other and did little jigs in the aisles. Some of the wives raised their skirts and did the cancan or the hula for little groups of whistling fools off to the side. They grabbed each other, felt each other, rolled their eyes and screeched like banshees. 'I've got a million dollars in my pocket,' I said. 'And some day each one of you wonderful guys and gals is going to have the same!' That started it again. Pandemonium! While it was going on, I had visitors on the stage. I was hugged and kissed. I was tickled and rubbed. A wife squeezed my crotch. Her husband ate a handful of confetti before my eyes. 'We're going to have *ten thousand* franchisers, we're going to take the Bully Burger overseas, we're going to teach the Pygmy, the Mandarin, and the Swami how to take the family out for dinner for under two dollars!' I told them.

"I was a big man, Claude, with a big appetite, and that million dollars I told them about wasn't in idle dreams. I *had* it, and they *knew* I had it, and they knew I'd get more. They had faith in me. I had promotional schemes that made them whistle and stomp. They knew I was a winner and they wanted the knack to rub off on them. Wives would come to my suite. I had carnal relations with more than a dozen of them. Sometimes two, three at once. There were no problems. The husbands knew all about it, probably sent them over. Each wife made double sure I got her name. The more industrious ones wrote it down. Penny Inez Fite. Marva Soapley. Diane Messerschmidt. I remember the ambitious ones best. I felt like a sultan. I *was* a sultan. The sultan of chopped beef. The sheik of buns. The pharaoh of french fries.

"We wound it up on a Sunday morning. It was a quiet farewell breakfast. I tapped my water glass for attention. 'Well, folks,' I said, 'we've had ourselves a *time*.' They applauded, but the applause was weak and modest. They were played out. They remembered all at once, in the clear light of Sunday morning, who they were. They knew they were going back to their little burger stands to put in that twelve-hour shift, seven days a week. They knew they were going back to the nitpicking worries of making ends meet: would that scatterbrained clown they hired last week work out? Would the public react negatively to the puffballs on his neck? Should they buy that new speaker system so that orders could be called in by the tenth car in line? Should they go to a twenty-four-hour day? Should they push apple turnovers? I looked at their faces. They were smiling. But the smiles were a little forced, a little pathetic. Distracted. Some may have had some mean thoughts about me at the time. 'The old bushwhacker is going to pep us up with his million-dollar ballyhoo and me ten dollars overdrawn at the First National!' Well, you can understand it. I also thought I detected a little tension here and there between hubby and wife. Well, you can easily understand that, too. There's a letdown after every party, right? And I knew that. I'd seen it before. This wasn't my first convention of franchisers. Yet something was happening to me. I didn't know what it was at the time. I opened my mouth to go on with my little speech, but nothing came out of it. I was going to tell them how to make their own luck, how hard work is only a part of the answer, when I all at once went blank. I mean *blank*. It was scary. I had to think hard for a minute to remember my own name. I guess they noticed it. Their smiles disappeared and they looked away. I mopped my face with my napkin. You could hear the fried eggs getting stiff. You could hear the ice melting in the water glasses. You could hear the sun climbing over the desert.

"It was *weird*, Claude. It was like something had come into that dining room that no one had expected. Something lethal. Picture king cobras under the tables, pythons in the chandeliers, tarantulas under the napkins. I just stood there with my mouth open. My franchisers began to get worried. They looked at each other and around the room. *They* sensed it too. A thing was present. Wives began to pat their lips with their napkins. Husbands shoved their plates away. Hearts began to pick up speed. And through it all, I could not speak a word.

"Some time later I thought of it as a vision, though that wasn't entirely correct. It was more of a perturbation, which is always the beginning of a vision, or at least it *can* be the beginning of one, though more often than not it's the beginning of a five-day drunk or a quick turn into a bridge abutment at ninety-five. All right. Picture this sudden and dangerous silence. And at a convention of laughers and talkers, believe me, sudden silence *is* dangerous. You get the feeling that if it stays quiet long enough anything will happen. Anything. Like the chairs might walk away, the knives might start humming through the air, the floors might turn into ooze. Anyway, whatever it was, it was taking hold and sucking something out of us. Picture a lamprey of the spirit. I think I must have started turning white or blue, because a woman stood up all at once and screamed. Everyone was thankful that she did, because that broke the spell. They all rushed to her side and pretended that *she* was the one that was in trouble and that *they* were the ones who could offer help, when in fact we all needed as much help as we could get just then. Well, we all went home after that but the memory of what had happened was strong in me. I couldn't concentrate on business. I had the doldrums. My secretary was handling the whole enterprise for me. But, naturally, she couldn't make the big decisions, the commitments. To get down to the short strokes, Claude, I went belly-up in a year, flat busted, kaput. The Bully Burger did a swan dive and flopped. Those two hundred ambitious young dildoes disappeared overnight and the bills and the lawsuits began to pour in. I filed for bankruptcy, gave my secretary a month's pay out of my own pocket, and dropped out of sight for good. A few years later I settled down here in Solar Flats to think and sort things out."

Bully ended his story. We sat for a long time just letting the swing move back and forth slowly. It got dark. The moon was higher and no longer orange. It was white as a plate. I could see mountain ranges, plateaus, seas of dust. My eyes are very good.

"I guess you know just what that lamprey in the dining room was," said Bully.

I did. I understood the Fable well. "D.D.T.," I said.

"That's right," said Bully. "Those two hundred hayseeds were breathing lungfuls of it and didn't know why they were feeling bad."

My eleventh painting is called *Full Moon over Solar Flats*, my twelfth is called *The Lamprey*, and the thirteenth will be a self-portrait: *Claude*.

The fog has come in from The Green Sea. It rubs against the large windows. From the patio gate I cannot see the pool. From the pool I cannot see the inside walls of the condominium. It is noon but the sun is buried. The sky is uniformly gray and the TV antennas disappear into it uniformly.

I am alone. Tellenbeck has gone to the University. For what possible reason I cannot say. Connie is in Solar Flats. Marlene is with Zip. There is nothing to do. The exercise room is cold and dismal. I am cold and my bones ache slightly, but I do not want to sit in the sauna or under the lamps.

I go back to the apartment. It is quiet. I turn on the TV. I look at the canvas. It is not going well. It is my tenth attempt at self-portrait. Something is wrong with the eyes, the brow, and the shape of the mouth. It is disturbing. I cannot show it to Marlene for her help. She has offered but I have said no thank you. I do not know why, but she must not see what the mouth is doing. She must not see the patterns of shadow on the brow.

I fall on the bed and roll over, laughing. I am laughing because everything that is happening now has happened before. I feel it so clearly. I remember that I am supposed to be frightened. But I am laughing. I go to the refrigerator and take out the bottle of yellow pills. I pour three into my hand. I fill a glass full of water. I let the pills slide between my fingers and into the garbage disposal. I drop the glass.

There are others becoming present. One, two, three, four, five, six, materializing in the air. A Female is showing her Tits to a stooped man. The man is reciting formulae. I smell fresh-baked bread. I hear frying. I taste copper pennies.

An old man is reading to me. "Those dildos play for keeps," he says, looking up from his book. "They bring their pet nightmare and they sniff your blood." He puts his arm around me and speaks into my ear. His breath is cold and moist like the fog. "One who hates rain," he says, "can wear a goddamned mackintosh over her evening gown and carry an umbrella. Her dildo boyfriend can bring a nice box of candy, which, when opened, will reveal a matched pair of green turds." He cackles, then brings his lips closer to my ear. "Listen," he hisses. "The paper snake will point right at their secret horror." He pulls me away from the rest and we go into the workshop. "But don't trust them farther than you can kick them," he says. "Give me your *oath* on this."

There is a humorous imbalance in the room and I cannot stop laughing and turning smartly again and again on my heel. Then I am at the switching panel. I turn on the biosaw. I grip the handles and slice the old man in half.

"Why did you do *that*, dildo?" he asks.

But I am barking hard with laughter and cannot answer. His legs dance away from his torso. I turn on the biostrobe, to tame his neurons. He flaps his arms and the torso flies around the room like a gull. I catch his shirttails and throw him into the emulsifier where he will become one liter of cellglue. I reach for the legs but they dance away from me.

The Female is in my room. She is on the bed. Her Tits shimmer in the strobing rainbows from the TV set. "Rupture me," she says. "Rupture me big."

I am lying on my back in the patio exploding goo.

Steady painful noise, rising. Water over rock clattering downhill sharply white and blades of blue lifting up and dropping down and the little boat quickly cleavered, then turning over as one by one its parts disappear before the river opens into the flatness of a lake where it is quiet momentarily and then the sound of crying Females and rifles in the trees, where you can see the wink wink of the well-aimed shots over the call of the hunting horns while the wind clicks in the dry trees *tickticktick* though the cabin where we are is tight and warm and always shall, mother, be safe.

Someone Else.

All of them wish me harm. "You must leave now," I say. They are not moving. They look at me and smile but their smiles are not friendly. They are eating bread with their mouths open in an attempt to disgust me. They are lounging in the kitchen as if they are within their rights but they are not within their rights. One of them stands by the light switch turning it on and off, slowly at first, then faster and faster. Then so fast it is strobing. "Go!" I say, but they do not move.

I am weak. I try to lift them one by one. They do not

move. I have no strength. I am frightened. My heart is beating fast but weak and I do not feel the volume of blood. I look at my arm, my beautiful bicep, but it is withering, becoming prune. I am crying hard. Sobbing. "*Go!*" I shout. But they do not. They strap me to the table. They turn on the biodrill and focus it on my chest. I am screaming.

One by one my muscles are removed. The Female drops them, white and knit with red, into the emulsifier.

I am alone. I cannot move. They have revived the Fly. They have made him large and strong. He moves around the room slowly as if he does not see me strapped here. But he does. He sees. He lands on the table and rubs and rubs his horrible legs. He crawls over my bones. He looks into my face. My soft sighs do not deter him. I am whispering for Tellenbeck. The Fly does not care. The Fly is as big and fierce as a hand. He crawls on my lips. He grooms his wings. He eats my eyes.

I am reading a cruel story about a famous international beauty who had everything to live for. "She was blessed with looks, love, wealth, and luck," says the article. "Then, at age thirty, a brain tumor reduced her to cole slaw. A year later she died. Her mother and close friends said, "That's not our Judy. That's a form of vegetable life.' They showed eight-millimeter films of the real Judy at the funeral." The article compares the famous beauty to a man who lived to be one hundred and sixteen. "The old geezer's life was filled with hard luck, sickness, and personal tragedy. He never had more than a hundred dollars in the bank at the same time. On his deathbed he slandered the day he was born."

I am reading about the evolution of the cerebral hemispheres, the limbic system, the basal ganglia, the interbrain, the midbrain, the cerebellum, the pons, the medulla, the spinal cord. It is like an exciting fiction told by a writer who cannot speak in short syllables.

A wife found her husband with another Female. She shot him with a pistol. The bullet severed his spinal cord, just below the neck. The man became totally paralyzed except for his facial muscles, which he learned to use for communication. The wife went to prison for six months and when she came out she had to nurse him for the next twenty-two years of his life. In that time she never once admitted regretting her act. "He learned to meditate," she said. "He learned the deeper significance of life. Our marriage had never been happier, even the honeymoon part."

The brain stem looks like an umbrella handle, or a question mark, or a big, hooking hitchhiker's thumb.

I am resting in the sun, by the pool, reading. I feel fine. I am strong. I am well. There is no problem. Yet Tellenbeck has made a rule: No more introspection. On lonely days I am to watch TV or exercise. "You have a tendency to become morbid and self-indulgent, Claude," he says. I do not think so. "Read magazines, talk to girls, shadow box, but, for Christ's sake, stop *thinking*."

He has locked up my paints. He saw my attempted

self-portrait and became very agitated. "That doesn't look like *you*, Claude. That's a terrible likeness," he said. I admit it is off the mark. Yet, Tellenbeck remains upset. "The eyes are not set right, Claude," he said. "The lips look like knuckles. The scars *show*."

Tellenbeck sees my painting as evidence of morbid introspection. He is wrong. When I paint I sing. I whistle. I am happy. I feel fine. I am well. There is no problem. I am reading about a man who changed jobs ninety-six times. He is now shoeing horses. Before horse-shoeing he was a book salesman. Before selling books he sold lamps. He had been married fifteen times, three times to the same wife. He changed his name from Doc to Hank, from Hank to Lobo, from Lobo to Kenny, from Kenny back to Doc. "When I was Doc, I made money," he said, "but when I was Lobo they chased me out of towns." He said he did it for the thrill. He liked his new wives to call him by a different name. Once he married a man on a dare. The man's name was Yancey. He made the man change his name from Yancey to Bleeder. "Change, change and more change," he said. "I guess I'm hooked on it. Some guys like booze or dope. Me, I get shitfaced on a quick change of itinerary." He worked as a supervisor in a tuna cannery. He was an unsuccessful politician for a time. Once he held up a laundromat for thirty-six dollars. "You reach a point in your life," he said, "when everything that's ever happened to you begins to seem unreal. That's when I say, *So long, suckers!*"

I am reading *Jack and the Beanstalk*. I have hidden the book of Fables between the covers of a large magazine because Tellenbeck thinks my love for it is symptomatic of the problem.

I close my eyes and I can hear the giant in the field grunting.

There is no problem.

Tellenbeck will not look at me. When he speaks he looks down or he looks at the ceiling. At the table he fiddles with the toaster or he reads. He seems nervous. Perhaps he is worrying about his future. He leaves every morning at nine and returns in mid-afternoon. He says he is "job hunting." But he wears the same wrinkled suit and his tie is stained. Sometimes he leaves without shaving or even brushing his teeth, his hairpiece set too far back on his head or off to one side. He is not neat as a pin or sharp as a tack. A prospective employer would take one look and then look elsewhere. Yet, I do not mention his appearance to Tellenbeck.

Today I pressed three hundred and ten pounds. I put the bar down and then picked it up and pressed it again.

After my sauna I step on the scales: two hundred and thirty-four pounds. I am not certain, but I think I have increased in height as well. Tellenbeck said the skeleton would not grow appreciably, but I believe it has. I am six feet four inches now. I do not think I was more than five feet eleven in the beginning.

No. I will not pose for her uncovered though she says please and does nice things for me. I know now that my Luigi is a staggering anomaly. It is too dark and its shape is all wrong according to the anatomy book. And it is far too large, though, in her view, this is a remarkable asset, a point of pride. Still, it is, for me, a source of extreme embarrassment. I do not understand Tellenbeck's motives in this. I have not expressed my annoyance to him. Some day I will.

I will not allow her to examine it closely. The shades must be drawn and the lights must be out and the covers must be on the bed at all times. Sometimes her fingers subtly trace its outline when I become incautious or doze. I take her wrist in my hand and make her stop. Sometimes she giggles, sometimes she winces, sometimes she scratches back or cries.

She must lie still and hold the covers over her face while I dress or undress. When I begin she must keep her eyes on the ceiling or close them. When I am finished she must hold her hands over her eyes while I rise.

When she peeks, I grow angry.

Yesterday I destroyed a chair.

"What are you *doing*, Claude?" she asked. She was frightened. She ran out of the room and hid from me.

"I am very angry," I said.

I took the legs off the chair one by one and then the arms and then I splintered the seat with my fists. Next time it will be a lamp or the dresser or the bed itself. She must not peek.

Tellenbeck has bought me a new outfit. It is very attractive. "It's called a tux, Claude," he says.

I put it on. The coat is white and very wide at the shoulders. The shoulders are padded. I look at myself in the mirror. I seem as wide as the door itself. I put on the trousers and then the shoes. The shoes are odd.

"Lifts," says Tellenbeck. "Designed to put a few inches on your height." I stand and I rise past the top of the mirror. I look down on Tellenbeck.

"I do not understand," I say.

"It's the latest fashion," says Tellenbeck. "I want you to feel stylish, okay?" Tellenbeck adjusts my tie. He has to reach high with his arms to do it. I stand back from the mirror so I can see myself fully. It is difficult to walk in these shoes. There is an imbalance and I must walk stiff-legged with my arms out from my sides for equilibrium.

"Beautiful," says Tellenbeck. "Just beautiful."

We are going someplace. Tellenbeck is driving the van. He has not told me where or why. He is smiling and cheerful for the first time in weeks but he will not say what for. It is the first time in weeks he has chosen a clean suit without wrinkles, a shirt without stains. It is a welcome change. I am very pleased.

He is whistling with energy and tapping his fingers on the steering wheel. He glances from time to time at me, quickly, as if to reassure himself of something, and when I try to meet his glance, he turns away and his whistling increases in volume.

Then I recognize streets and the jutting rise of buildings. We are among the towers and low square structures of State Polytechnic University. Tellenbeck parks the van. He gets out. I do not.

"Well, come *on*, Claude," he says. I look at him.

"Why are we here?" I ask. He opens my door. I close it. He opens it again. I close it and lock it.

"Claude, for Christ's sake, I just want you to help me with a *crate*. It's packed with some of my instruments." I look at him. "I need a big strapping fellow like you, and on my unemployment pay I sure can't afford to hire someone." He is smiling at me.

I feel foolish and petty. I am ashamed. "All right," I say, and get out.

We take the elevator to the sixth floor of one of the white towers. "You know," says Tellenbeck as we are walking down the hall, "I miss this place. I even miss some of the noodles who work here. Ungaretti, Schroeder, Isozu."

There is a large door at the end of the hall. There is a red sign above it. AUDITORIUM. "This was my eighth university, Claude," says Tellenbeck. "I had always hoped it would be my last."

We reach the door. "Just walk in, Claude, and don't stop until I say so."

Tellenbeck opens the door and I enter. There are many bright lights and I have to shield my eyes. There are many voices. I hear scattered applause and I remember the finger stand but I have no impulse to do it. I hear nervous laughter. I turn and look at Tellenbeck. "Keep moving," he whispers. He nods to someone and smiles. His hand is in the small of my back and I am walking stiff-legged with reluctance. My eyes adjust, finally, to the light and I see that we are on a stage of some kind. There is an audience. There are TV cameras and microphones hanging above the stage. Tellenbeck is holding my hand.

"Sit here, Claude," he says. There are three chairs side by side.

"Where is the crate with your instruments?" I ask. I am suspicious.

"Later, *later*," he says quickly. A man sits next to us and counts to ten into a microphone. He attaches a microphone to my lapel. I take Tellenbeck's wrist and squeeze it hard.

"What is the purpose . . . ?" I ask. I am confused and uneasy. There is something wrong.

"Hey, Tellenbeck," someone from the audience calls out. The voice is cruel and grating but I cannot see where it originates. The faces blur together and they are all the same. A single creature with a thousand faces. And then I see something move among the faces, quick and invisible. Tellenbeck is coughing nervously and searching himself for a cigarette. "Hey, Tellenbeck," the grating voice calls out again. "Is that your monster?"

The word strikes me hard. I rise an inch and clench my teeth. I make a sound deep in my throat and close my eyes. I bring my fists to my ears. The word echoes like repeated blows from a hammer and the nail of pain is driven in deeper and deeper behind my ear, splitting the brain. The word has become a pain word. The word has become a pain word!

"All right," says the man in the third chair. "We're on the air in fifteen secs, people."

I look at the man. He does not see my tears. I take off the microphone and hand it to him. I stand up and leave the stage. I am walking stiffly with my arms held out from my sides for balance. Tellenbeck comes after me. I hear a great roar of laughter. I hear catcalls, boos and crude whistling. A rhythmic, disdainful clapping escorts us off the stage.

"Stop, goddamn you, Claude! Stop!" says Tellenbeck. "I'm doing this for your own good! We need the money. We have to go public. Another week might be too late. The diapause . . ."

"I do not need money," I say.

Tellenbeck is hanging on my arm and trying to prevent me from entering the elevator. I pick him up by the waist. "Put me down, you stupid grunt!" he shouts. I have to grin bitterly to myself. So, that is what he truly thinks of me. Somehow, I am not surprised. Somehow, I am not surprised at all.

I carry him out of the building and across the parking lot. I place him in the van. I connect his seat belt and shoulder harness. I cinch them tight.

"Crate," I say, as I turn the van into the street. "Instruments," I say, accelerating. I drive down the ramp and merge into the freeway traffic and slide over to the speed lane and put the speedometer on eighty. *"Strapping fellow,"* I say, letting the full irony of these words ring in his ears.

"So, THAT is where you have been going every morning," I say. Tellenbeck is not speaking to me. "You have been making arrangements for a public announcement."

Tellenbeck is biting at the ropes but his teeth are dull and weak. Old and soft.

"Of course, your colleagues did not believe you, and so you went to the news media knowing that they would gladly help you arrange it because the public is bored and always has an appetite for bizarre stories."

Tellenbeck is growling like a dog but he cannot sever a strand of the macramé net. Later, I will fashion it into a proper cage with wooden beams to hold the ropes.

"You knew, of course, that they would have locked me in a room, examined me at will, probed me, perhaps even dissected me, that they would have, in fact, done anything to me that pleased their scientific curiosity. Once it was made clear that I have no rights as a Person I would have been no better off than the dogs and cats they use in their vivisection laboratories. And you, Doctor Tellenbeck, knew that."

Exhausted, Tellenbeck lies back on the cushions I have provided for him. We are in the workshop.

"And to think," I say, "that in the beginning I was sorrowful because I could not be filial to you." Anger and resentment surge powerfully in me and I take a step toward him. He moves quickly, like a crab, but I stop short of the ropes. "You, Tellenbeck, have always regarded me as Alpha Six, the successful experiment, and never as a Person."

"*Monster,*" Tellenbeck says.

My head snaps back. I put my fists to my temples. The word caught me by surprise in the auditorium, and now, once again, in the workshop. Tears spill down my face.

"*Monster, monster, monster,*" he says, louder each time, his face vicious and deranged.

"Naarr," I say in my agony, staggering back. "Naaarrr."

I leave the room slamming the door behind me. I go into the bathroom where I vomit suddenly and with violence. The pain is severe. I take aspirin from the medicine chest and swallow half a bottle. I go into my room and turn on the TV so that the word will be drowned out. I lie down on the bed. There is a situation comedy on with a disproportionately loud laugh track. I try to enjoy the antics of the husband and wife who are wrestling with a buttered seal in their kitchen, but the tears will not stop.

I doze and when I wake Someone Else is waking with

me. It is sharper than memory. It is stronger than image. The sharp taste of copper pennies fills my mouth and I drool.

I slide out of bed and fall forward on my hands. I walk out of the room on my hands. It is enjoyable. I am thinking the word *who*. Who. Who. Who. And the word *Carlos* moves my tongue. Several words in a language I do not understand move across the surface of my mind. They are like small birds darting between trees, too quickly to be identified. "*Bueno*," I say, aloud. "*Bueno, compañero.*"

It passes and I stand. The blood rushes out of my head and there is a strong imbalance. I lean against a table. I breathe deeply. I do ten deep knee bends. I expand my chest. I let the released air flutter my lips. The imbalance passes.

I leave the apartment and the memory of the day's unpleasantness behind me. I walk to the pool. It is a bright and sunny day, warm and fragrant. I expand my chest. Connie is by the pool.

"Hello hello," I say. She shades her eyes and looks up at me.

"Oh, hello, Claude," she says. Then she raises herself on her elbows. "A tuxedo?" she asks.

I put my thumbs under the lapels and rise on my toes. "How do you like it?" I ask.

"Scrumptious," she says. "Adorable. But the shoulders . . ."

I decide to go up to Marlene's apartment. I ring six

times before she answers. She is in a robe and her hair is not arranged.

"Claude, you stinker," she says. Zip Porter is be nd her. He is wearing a bathrobe too.

"Hey," he says. "Crude timing, sport."

Marlene makes tea and we sit at the kitchen table. "Well," says Zip. "You going to tell us what the occasion is?"

"Occasion?" I ask.

"The tux, Claude," says Marlene.

"My uncle," I say, "wanted me to look nice. *Sharp* he said."

Marlene looks at me with an expression I have seen only in her bedroom. "Well, *yum*," she says.

"He is a cute little bugger, isn't he?" says Zip, but his smile is like wax.

"But I thought shoulder pads went out a century ago," says Marlene.

I sip my tea. And then Someone Else is there again. This time it is overpowering and frightening. I must tell Tellenbeck. But I cannot tell him anything any longer. It is too late for that.

I am making fists. I am looking first at Marlene and then at Zip. *It is clear they have had the whole treat.* I am looking for chairs to destroy.

"What is it, Claude?" Marlene asks.

I do not answer. I am compressing my lips. I am grinding my teeth. I taste my own blood. I am visualizing her bedroom ten minutes ago. I am remembering the sound she makes when it is over. *aaooon.* I stand up stiffly, each muscle flexed and quivering with blood pressure. My neck is bulging against my shirt collar. My systole is over two hundred. I am so powerful at this moment I could easily pick them up and push them through the walls.

"Jesus," says Zip. "You having a fit or something?" He looks nervous and frightened.

I move toward him one inch then force myself to stop. *Stop,* I tell the Someone Else, for this rage is not mine. *Do not. These are my friends.* But the Someone Else releases dozens of harsh words and phrases I do not understand. *Stop, stop.* But he does not choose to understand my words. I force myself to spin around on my heel and walk to the front door. I have to spin full circle several times before I reach it, my back arched and stiff, my lungs rigid with determination. But his rage is flying in my blood. The impulse to crush bones, rend flesh, and let blood is strong.

Castrado, says the Someone Else scornfully. *Cabrón.*

"*Adiós,*" I say, over my shoulder, trying to make my voice pleasant and friendly, trying to smile, but failing. "*Adiós,* you tricky bastardinos."

I bring Tellenbeck food while he sleeps. I will not endure the pain words he utters whenever he sees me. Once he pretended to be asleep and as I set the tray next to his cage, he said, "*Klystron,*" very loudly into my ear. I struck him. It was the first time I have ever struck another. I cried from the pain and from the humiliation. He staggered away from the blow and crawled into a corner of the cage. I saw blood in his mouth.

I have found his notes. They are mostly indecipherable. Sometimes he lapses into clear prose. In these passages I make discoveries about myself. Some of the discoveries are interesting. My eyes are from a Female donor named Alberta Brownlee. My ears once belonged to a Charles K. Nesbitt. The brainpan once provided a canopy for the thoughts of one Billy C. J. Blizzard. There is no record of the brain itself.

I have found my paints and canvases. I set up my easel in the living room near the large window. It is a fine studio. I decide to paint several seascapes before attempting to return to my self-portrait. Tellenbeck tries to disturb my concentration. I hear him shouting and pounding. If he is uttering pain words I am not able to make them out. I have lined the walls of the workshop with heavy blankets for acoustic insulation. It works quite well. When I bring him food, I am careful to wear the stereo earphones I have purchased. They are large and the padding is excellent. I have connected them to a long cord which is plugged into a small tape machine. When I feed him, I play symphonic music at a high volume. Mozart. Wagner. Beethoven. Brahms. I like it. I hear nothing but the music. I see his vocal cords straining. I see his face becoming red with effort. But it does not bother me in the least. I place his corn flakes or his cheese sandwiches in front of him and pour him a glass of milk. I have allowed him a small ration of alcohol. At first he would knock everything over and sulk. But he grew hungry. He grew thirsty. He does not eat or drink until I have left the workshop. But he eats and drinks everything when I am gone. When I bring in his tray I see his eyes fill with hatred. They grow red and blind with anger. Though they never saw, they now see less.

I might have been filial once. Had he let me.

I have used one of Tellenbeck's charge cards to purchase a large TV set which has incorporated into it a video tape recorder. I have recorded several of my favorite movies and now watch them when I please. It is wonderful. I have six Claude Rains films. I am studying his mannerisms and his speech. The way he raises his eyebrows. The way he smiles, as if he has special knowledge of an enduring sadness but has learned to accommodate it with good humor and a civilized disposition. He is small and frail and I am large and powerful, but I do not think our qualities of mind are far removed from each other. At least I like to think they are not.

The despicable truth is on page one hundred and twenty-six of Tellenbeck's notes. *Despicable*.

As Alpha-6's member, I have chosen that of a Shetland stud,

a feisty little stallion named Luigi. The testes are from a nine-year-old mountain gorilla by the amusing name of Sig. I have not done this out of showmanship or from a malignant twist of imagination, but as a method of presenting to the unbeliever a quick, *external* proof. For this purpose, the genitals were more practical than, say, the ears or feet.

N.B. They will suggest dissection, of course, to retrace each step, but this *I shall not allow*. (Except as a last resort.)

The idea is wonderful! To express it, I have stretched a very large canvas:

The fog is close. Perhaps one hundred yards from the shore. And the sun is in the center of it. The sun is a luminous green oblate sphere, not millions of miles beyond the horizon, but buried in fog, perhaps only a few hundred feet deep. Three careful long-legged birds stand on the gray sand. I have made their eyes large and white, reflecting small green suns. White water slides toward their feet. The sky is slate but giving an overpowering impression of thinness. It is a brittle dome, ready to crack. The observer finds himself looking for cover within a glazed egg. He looks with justified alarm at the tension in the fragile shell.

I am swimming. I am very cold. I am awake. I have swallowed several mouthfuls of salt water and I feel nauseous. I did not know I was a swimmer. I did not know I was powerful in the water. My strokes are steady and strong. But I do not know why I am swimming.

I went to bed. The Late Movie was boring. I slept. I

dreamed a new dream. It was a dream of painting. A masterpiece was forming on the canvas. I was applying paint with my fists. Then I awoke, here in The Green Sea, surrounded by fog. Then I remember Tellenbeck's word for the dysfunction. Somnambulism.

I hear the surf but I cannot tell its direction. I swim and it grows fainter. I reverse my direction and it increases in volume. Then I am swimming among large rocks in violent water. I am thrown against a rock and dazed. I crawl toward the beach, through the weight of collapsing breakers. I rest in the cold sand. I am still wearing my pajamas.

I am not far from The Sun Spot. It is still dark. When I am back in the apartment I take a warm bath to restore heat to my body. I do not like to be cold.

I look in on Tellenbeck. He is lying on the mattress I have provided for him. He is snoring. I see that he has emptied the jar of alcohol. I give him six ounces every evening. I check the ropes of his cage to make sure he has not managed to fray any of them. They are intact. I tiptoe out and return to bed.

I am afraid to go to sleep. I decide to tie my foot to the bed frame with a length of stout rope.

Marlene is overwhelmed. She is looking at my new painting and cannot believe her eyes. She sits down on the couch and puts her hands to her face. "Lordy," she says. "Let me get my bearings."

"I call it *Locked Views*," I say.

"Incredible," she says. "*Prophetic.*"

I do not understand what she means by that.

"It has a prophetic *quality*," she explains. "Apocalyptic vibes. It gives me the shivers, Claude. I love it." I am pleased.

"We'll need to set up a show for you. You're getting too good to be kept under wraps."

At first the idea is exciting. Then frightening. "No," I say. "No show."

Marlene looks at me with disbelief on her face. "What do you mean, no *show?*" she asks. "You'll be a smash, Claude. They'll *love* you. You'll make a fortune. I suppose you're going to tell me that money means nothing to you. Claude, I don't want to *hear* that bullshit."

"It is not a sunset at sea," I say.

"You're goddamned right it isn't," she says. "I'm not talking about a rinky-dink set-up in The Center, on the mall with all the pushcarts and balloons. I'm talking about the posh galleries. I'm talking about traveling shows. I'm not talking thirty or forty dollars a canvas. I'm talking five *hundred*, a thousand, *two* thousand. I'm talking about a reputation that will be worth its weight in lectureships at the best art schools."

Her arguments are strong. The problem of money has occurred to me. Tellenbeck can no longer be depended upon for an income. I have been using his charge cards but soon the requests for payment will begin to arrive and I will have to satisfy them. But selling my paintings is not the way. It is unthinkable. They are gifts from my hand to my eye. There are things in them that I need to understand. They are very much like the Fables in that way.

"No," I repeat. "No shows."

Marlene is very upset. She cannot understand my reluctance.

"Please do not be angry with me, Marlene," I say.

"Oh, shit with it," she says, and leaves.

I go into the workshop and untie Tellenbeck's hands and feet. I remove the gag from his mouth. He is asking me, with a sneer on his face, if my company has left.

"Yes," I answer.

He points to my ears. I shake my head. He cannot be trusted. He forms the word *please* with his lips and assumes a begging posture. He is filled with mocking irony and cannot be trusted. I would be a fool to remove the earphones. Besides, the *Tannhäuser* overture is on right now, one of my all-time favorites.

Tellenbeck is on his hands and knees pretending to lick the floor. He holds his hands together and closes his eyes in a vulgar parody of prayer. He bounces on his haunches and hooks his fingers into his mouth and exposes all his teeth like a baboon. But I will not be harassed by these stupid antics. I turn to leave, and then his pleas become serious. His eyes are wide and frightened. It has been three weeks. He points excitedly to my ears.

"No," I say. "You cannot be trusted."

He forms the word *please* again. I shake my head no. Then an idea occurs to me. I go to my room and get my crayons. I get several sheets of thick construction paper. "Write what you want to say to me with these," I say. Tellenbeck shrugs, but he takes the crayons and paper.

How long? he writes.

"How long what, Doctor Tellenbeck?"

Jail.

"I haven't thought about it."

Think about it.

"You cannot be trusted, Doctor. You fibbed. You tried to bring me before the TV cameras. You tried to make a public spectacle of me."

Sorry about that, Claude.

"Are you?" I do not believe him for a minute.

Yes. Truly. Sorry. Honest.

"Ha ha ha," I say, but I am not laughing. Then he begins to write furiously.

Claude, remember when I had to carry you like a baby from room to room? Remember how you used to fear the movements of your bowels and how I had to hold your hand and dry your tears? Remember when you first opened your eyes and saw the flowers I had placed next to your bed? I wanted you to think of me as your father, Claude. I asked you to call me Kraft. You remember? But you refused. You rejected me. YOU REJECTED ME. Who was acting in bad faith in those days, Claude? Who wouldn't lift a finger in a simple act of friendship

*back in the days when you were so totally dependent on
old Tellenbeck? You remember? You remember when
the shoe was on the other foot?*

"Does a father turn his son over to the butchers?" I
ask.

Tellenbeck breaks a crayon. He has nothing more to
write. He rises and throws himself against the ropes of
his cage. He rebounds sharply from the ropes and falls
to the floor. I leave before he begins his tiresome begging.

I pour myself a second glass of Riesling. I have come
to like it as much as ginger ale. It improves my mood. I
pick up the phone and dial seven random numbers. A
Female answers. "I want to tell you some remarkable
scientific facts concerning myself," I say, in Claude
Rains's voice.

"All right," says the Female.

I read her pages one hundred and ten through one
hundred and seventeen in Tellenbeck's notebook.

"What does 'labiact' mean?" she says. "It sounds rotten dirty."

"It is an acronym for Laser Biotronic Actinism," I say.

"I'll bet," she says. "But tell me more about yourself,
hon. Your politics, special interests, hobbies, perhaps a
filthy secret or two."

I tell her about the Fables. I tell her about the giant
Female and the giant who cannot understand that he is
thoroughly despised in the castle.

"So far, so good," she says.

I tell her my Luigi is too long and thick as a branch and once belonged to a little stallion.

"Socko," she says.

I pour myself another glass of wine. The sun is nearly blue behind the oily smoke of a passing steamer. The world is beautiful and sad. Blue, cupped in haze. Warmth, bled by infinite cold. So touching, so melancholy. I have an urge to sing, but I do not know how.

"The shoemaker and his wife decided to sit up one evening to see who had surreptitiously helped them manufacture shoes," I say into the tape recorder. "At midnight two little naked men came in and began to stitch leather."

I dial another group of seven numbers. *"Now we're boys so fine and neat, why cobble more for others' feet?"* I say.

I hear a nervous flapping of wings, a rain of pebbles.

This is Zip's treat. We are in The Mean Pig, an elegant restaurant. Zip has ordered chateaubriand for all of us. There are large fireplaces. There are shields and swords on the walls. I am seated next to Connie and Zip is next to Marlene. We are drinking champagne. It is delicious. It is like ginger ale and Riesling combined. I borrow a pencil from Connie and write the brand name of the champagne on my cuff.

"I'm sure glad you're not sore at me," says Zip, smiling.

"Sore?" I ask.

"About the other day. You know, at Marl's." I look at Marlene. She raises her glass to her lips.

"I am not sore," I say.

"Boy, that's a relief," says Zip. "Wouldn't do to have a bruiserino like you sore at a fella."

After dinner we go to the bar.

"My treat," says Zip. "What are you drinking, Claude?"

"The Schramsberg Blanc de Blancs," I say, reading from my cuff.

"Give him a champagne cocktail," says Zip to the bartender.

A warmth slides down my throat and though I do not especially like the flavor of this drink I like the heat it creates deep within me. I have trouble keeping warm lately, especially in the evening after the sun goes down and the fog moves in.

Zip tells two jokes. The first is about a man and a mechanical garden. The second is about a mysteriously shrinking husband who sends anonymous threats to the surgeon general. Connie and Marlene laugh with exuberance. I thought I had learned humor well but in this instance my laugh is not genuine. I make a mental note to study the humor of jokes. I have read a large volume called *A Schematized History of Humor and Wit: 1775–1955*, but nothing in its one thousand pages has made me laugh.

A man takes Connie by the wrists as we are leaving the bar. "Let go," says Connie. The man does not. The man is smiling. His face is thin and sharp. It looks like it could cut paper. He is a small man and he appears to be very strong because Connie cannot free herself.

"What a pair," he says. He is looking at Connie's Tits. "Boing!" he says. He has been drinking alcohol and his mood is boisterous. I approach him. He looks at me. "Oh, the boyfriend," he says, sneering at me. "Going to give little Wally Hawks a lesson in front of Angel Tits?" he says.

"Let her go," I say. He is holding her wrists so tightly that Connie is wincing. I do not like to see her wince.

"Going to feed little Wally Hawks a knuckle sandwich, boyfriend?" he says, chuckling without humor. I touch his shoulder. His face suddenly becomes very white and his blue lips curl down. He opens his hands. Connie pulls away from him.

"Thank you," I say, and turn to leave.

Suddenly I am on the floor on my back next to the stools. Bright blue eggs are floating in front of my eyes. There is much pain. It is centered in my lower abdomen and radiating outward. I roll over and vomit chateaubriand and champagne.

"Oh Christolo," says Zip. "He had to get testy with a Kung Fu whiz."

I am on my hands and knees trying to breathe. I turn my head to see what has happened to me and the toe of a shoe enters my mouth. I roll into the barstools. I am swallowing large volumes of my own blood. A tooth fragment is on my lip. This is very disturbing. I am crying. Connie is next to me.

"The filthy *beast*," she says. She is crying too. Zip is trying to help me up. I do not feel well.

"What happened?" I ask. "Is this the Marbut Exit?"

My friends look puzzled. "Shock," says Zip. "He's in shock."

Marlene is wiping my face with a napkin. The little man with the thin face is standing just outside our circle, bouncing up and down on his toes. He is grinning cruelly. I begin to realize that I have been attacked and that my attacker is this little man with the sharp face.

A voice in my head says, *Cabrón*.

"What did you call Wally Hawks?" says the little bouncing man. I did not realize I uttered the strange word aloud.

"*Cabrón*," I repeat.

"That's a dirty word, boyfriend," he says. He crouches then and begins to come toward me. He is going to hurt me again. There is a sinister hunch in his shoulders. A murderous arch in his back. I am frightened.

"*Tronche su miembro, castrado*," says the voice. I do not understand the words, but there is a rage behind them that is moving outward. It is moving into my face and eyes. I can feel it in my arms and legs, in my fingers and toes. I hear it in my throat.

His fist strikes me on the forehead. His other fist goes into my neck. There is darkness. I am inside a great cavern of darkness. A cold wind is pouring in from above. Thin voices on wires thread down to me. Three faces emerge from the dark.

"Claude! Claude!" It is Connie. "Oh, God, he's been killed!" she says. She is holding my head. Marlene is wiping my face again. The napkin is wet and cold.

"Call the boys in blue," Zip says to someone I cannot see.

But I haven't been killed. Soon I am able to stand up with the help of my friends. A strong imbalance in the room makes it lean to the left and spin slightly.

"*Afeminado*," says the voice. The voice is thick with disgust.

"*Shut up*, you," I say aloud.

My friends look surprised. They look at each other. "Wally Hawks!" I shout. The little man is leaving the barroom. He turns.

"Oh, Jesus, Claude," says Zip.

I stagger to the right, trying to resist the room's tilt to the left. The little man dismisses me with a wave of his hand and turns again to leave.

Then I am running. Chairs and tables fly up in front of me and scatter to the side. My friends are shouting. Wally Hawks turns the instant before I reach him and I am flying through the air, grasping nothing more than a retinal memory of his neck, nothing to stop my flight but a large window of many panes. I crash through it and fall several feet through cool air and into a thick hedge.

I stay in the hedge, recovering. I am cut in several

places but not severely. I am shivering with Someone Else's rage and my own fear. Thoughts of revenge contend with thoughts of hiding in this hedge forever. The main entrance to The Mean Pig is at the end of the hedge. I crawl on my hands and knees toward the entrance, and wait. Wally Hawks comes down the steps. He dances down on clever little feet tugging smartly at his shirt cuffs and whistling gaily. I hate him. Not just for what he has done to me, but for what he is. For the first time, I wish to do real harm. I do not feel sweet.

When he is very close, I grasp him around the waist with both arms. A rain of fists falls on my head, but I keep my shoulders hunched protectively and lift him into the air. I am squeezing with all my strength. He makes a savage growling noise. Then I lift him high, transferring my left hand to the back of his neck and my right hand to the base of his spine. I press him easily. He weighs no more than one hundred and fifty pounds. He is writhing and kicking, but now he has no point of leverage. He is no longer in a position to do harm. I carry him back into The Mean Pig over my head at arm's length.

"You have the brain of a dog," I tell him. "And the heart of a weasel." Inside, I push him, as slowly as possible, through a wall.

I am taking my pulse and blood pressure but it is not myself that I am worried about, it is the TV. Two channels are inoperative. The video tape section is flawless, but I am worried that the infection will spread to it, eventually, if precautions are not taken. I put the ear of a stethoscope against the set. The correct hums are present and they appear healthy. But then I hear an electric tearing sound through the stethoscope. It lasts only a moment, a millisecond perhaps, but I take off the back of the set to see if it is visible, the dysfunction. I do not hear it again. And I do not see it.

Today, the garbage disposal coughed. I had filled it with nothing more than eggshells and orange peelings. And yet, a fine mist of peel and shell erupted from the hole and I sneezed violently several times. I removed the mechanism from the sink and took it apart. I scraped and cleaned each part. I oiled the bearings of the motor. Then I reassembled it and put it back into the sink. Later, it coughed on lettuce.

The van does not accelerate well between fifty-five and sixty. I have taken out the plugs, scraped them clean, gapped them, but the acceleration is still inferior.

What happened to your face? writes Tellenbeck. I held up my hand so that he would not see the damage, but he saw.

"I fell," I say, fibbing.

Tellenbeck is sitting back on his haunches and eating a head of lettuce.

Looks more like someone beat the crap out of you.

There is an evil gloat in his eyes. He no longer begs me to release him. He appears to be waiting for the worst to happen. He appears to believe that time is on

his side. He is wrong. He is wrong. Preventative maintenance will save machines, body and mind. Provided I
remain alert.

I am disturbed by the poor quality of fabric. I see little
threads breaking in my shirts. The carpets are becoming
frayed. Sunlight is destroying the curtains, decomposing
dye.

I tie and gag Tellenbeck and answer the door. It is
Marlene.

"Claude the hermit," she says.

"I have not been feeling up to par," I say, fibbing.

"Well, *Claude*," she says, touching my swollen face.

"I know," I say, looking down at my feet. "You are
my friend."

She laughs but there is a brittle edge to it. I look at
her closely. She seems pale and nervous. Out of sorts. I
do not like the dullness of her eyes. I sit next to her on
the couch.

"Claude," she says. "What are you *doing?*"

I am taking her pulse. "SShhh," I say. I wrap the inflatable sleeve around her arm. I pump it full of air. One-
thirty over ninety. "I think you drink too much coffee
and smoke too many cigarettes," I tell her. "Describe
your stool, please."

"*Claude!*" She tries to pull away from me but I hold
her still.

"Is it firm yet free of telltale lumpiness and does it
average over two hundred grams per deposit?" She rolls

her eyes. I see a yellowish tint. "Let me see your tongue," I say.

"No. Nothing doing," she says.

I take her jaw in my hand and squeeze. "Open," I say. She opens. There is a fine coating far back. Nothing serious. The taste buds, however, exhibit a symptomatic roughness. I go to the refrigerator and take out a small bottle. "Take these," I say. "One with each meal. B-complex. Do you a world of good." I put on my stethoscope and open her blouse.

"We have to be on our guard at all times," I say. "The threats are multiplying."

"Claude," she says, "you're crazy."

I am standing at the base of the hill looking up at The Sun Spot. Its construction seems suspect. In case of quake or high wind, all would collapse. I am sure of it. I have seen squat massive buildings of concrete and steel. These make sense to me. But bare wood and glass in odd and fragile arrangements do not. The threats are multiplying. There is danger.

Tellenbeck is looking at me and smirking.

The deep end, Claude.

I am listening to a soaring pipe-organ fugue. "You look peaked, Doctor Tellenbeck," I say.

You're coming unglued. Let me out. I can fix.

"It is not *I*," I say. "I am fine. It is *you*. Let me have a look at your tongue."

Nothing doing.

"Suit yourself, Doctor."

I go out to the kitchen and dial seven numbers with my eyes closed. An adolescent answers. "Tuberculosis of the bone marrow is on the increase," I say. The adolescent hangs up. I dial seven more numbers with my back to the phone. A Female answers. "Go on like you have been and it will be ulcerated colitis for certain." The Female hangs up. I turn the dial seven times with my elbow. A recording answers. "Mechanical breakdown due to inferior materials and indifferent workmanship is growing at an alarming rate," I say.

I strip down and look at myself in the mirror. My muscles are perfect. "Thank goodness for that," I say to my reflection. "Thank goodness that I, at least, am in superb condition and in no danger." I knock on wood three times. I print a large sign with the words *Preventative Maintenance* and hang it in my room.

I hang charts of the body. The bicep has a big red middle section shaped like a stomach and small, perhaps too small, white ends. These are called tendons. The middle of the bicep is its strength. But all its power comes to bear on the tendons. The tendon does not contract. It is pulled along by the bicep and the skeleton moves. The tendon is the muscle's hand. It holds the bone. But can it be trusted?

I sneeze often without warning. The sneeze involves the muscles of the abdominal wall and larynx. The larynx is forced to close and the abdominal muscles increase the pressure on the lungs though the diaphragm is passive. The larynx is snapped open like a trap and air is blown from the lungs with great force. The lungs are divided by the heart and arteries. There in the thoracic cavity lies the core of life. It is said that the sneeze stops the heart.

This is the visceral pleura, and this a pulmonary vein. Those are fissures. And there, below the ventricle, another fissure. It is called the oblique fissure.

And those at the ends of the bronchioles are called alveoli. Their delicacy saddens me. Tears well up in my eyes. The charts blur. The profound delicacy of the interior, the complex tubings and joinings, the careful spacing of organs under the cage of bones, fills me with melancholy and wonder.

But can any of it be trusted?

IT IS not my idea. It is Zip Porter's idea. It is a good idea. The wolf is at the door. I cannot go on using Tellenbeck's charge cards. The demands for payment are coming in. There have been threats of forcible collection. I have received cold notes from legal firms who specialize in the collection of overdue debts. I must have money.

We are in The Center. We are in the office of Burt

Butz. Burt Butz is the Chief of Security for The Center. He is wearing a gray uniform and a weapon. He is looking at me closely. I am remembering to smile. "A smile is your ticket to success," Zip told me. "That's how I got to where I am today. Smile and the world is your oyster. Let a smile be your umbrella on a rainy, rainy day." And so I am smiling. My teeth are white and good. They are strong and healthy. Except for a missing fragment of an upper incisor, they are perfect. "Teeth like yours, Claude, are money in the bank," says Zip.

"I don't see anything here about education," says Burt Butz, looking at the application form I have filled out. I wrote many fibs, but there were some questions I could not reply to because there are still holes in my knowledge.

"Private tutoring, right, Claude?" Zip says. It is not a fib.

"Yes," I say with enthusiasm, remembering to smile brightly. "My education has been with a tutor."

Zip leans toward Chief Butz and says, "Look, Burt, this boy is not *dumb*." Zip's voice is confidential, almost a whisper. I have to lean forward to hear his words. "*Uninformed*, maybe. A bit back-woodsy, perhaps. I mean, he doesn't know if Christ was crucified or died of the whiskey shits, Burt, but he is not what you would call *dumb*."

Burt Butz takes off his tinted glasses and squints at the ceiling. "No experience," he says.

"Right," says Zip. "Right right right. But a boy can learn, can't he? And besides, my man here has something we *need* on the mall."

Chief Butz puts his glasses back on and looks at Zip. "And just what would that be?" he asks. There is doubt in his voice and sourness in his face. His thumbs flick nervously with impatience.

"Well, think a minute, Burtolo, about the physical gifts Claude is offering us. I mean, what have you got *now?* A bunch of zombies, stick men, and walruses. It would take ten of those troopers to hold down a sixty-year-old grandma. Now, Claude, here, is a one-man riot squad. I've seen him in action. Claude, make a muscle for Burt."

I hold up my right arm and make the bicep jump. I am wearing short sleeves.

Burt Butz leans forward in his chair and touches my bicep with his swagger stick. He rubs his chin. He scratches his head. "Okay," he says. "I'll try him out. Report to my office tomorrow morning, Mr. Rains."

Zip pats me on the shoulder. I am very happy. The starting pay for a security guard is handsome. It is almost as much as Tellenbeck was receiving from the University. The uniforms are not included but the weapon is.

"Chief Butz is what you might call a first-water bastardino," says Zip when we are back on the mall. "But he knows good horseflesh when he sees it."

The smell of burnt meat makes me vomit. I run out of the workshop and barely make it into the bathroom. When I recover, I tie a handkerchief over my nose and mouth and re-enter the workshop.

Tellenbeck has hurt himself seriously. The biosaw is on and turning erratically, cutting black arcs into the ceiling and walls. The biodrill has melted a light switch. The biostrobe is making the room dance and blaze. I crawl on my hands and knees to the switching panel and turn off the machines. Tellenbeck is lying on his stomach, unconscious.

I see hardened blood. I see darkened flesh. The ropes of the cage have been cut several times over. I roll Tellenbeck to his back. I have to vomit again. Before I return to the workshop, I go into the kitchen and drink a glass of champagne. I refill the glass. The retinal memory of Tellenbeck's wound floats before me. I brush at the air before my eyes but it does not go away.

I return to the workshop. Tellenbeck has not moved. He is not dead, but he cannot possibly live much longer. The machines have split the skin, the corium, and the wall of muscle. I see the internal organs. I touch my forehead and close my eyes. I am trembling.

The wound is near the liver. I see the organ, brown-red and glistening. I see the soft intestines. The heat of the biosaw has cauterized the wound and the loss of blood has been minimal. As a consequence, Tellenbeck lives.

I did not believe he could reach the switches. I made sure of that. Then I see the food tray. Tellenbeck apparently threw it at the panel of switches, hoping that it would turn on one or more of the laser devices and that the beams would cut the ropes of his cage.

It worked.

I have spread antibiotic paste over the wound and wrapped it in sheets but it is useless. I have put him in his bed. There are moments when he is conscious or partially conscious. He asks me for water. He does not seem to recognize me. He calls me Tommy Freestone and says, "What a time we had, Tommy boy," and, "Blooey, Tom, the whole works went blooey."

When he speaks like this his eyes move as if from scene to scene and he does not realize I am in the room with him. It is distressing. I take his temperature and blood pressure every hour and they are not good. His pulse is fast and weak and sometimes I cannot find it at all. His hands and feet are cold and the coldness is creeping relentlessly up his limbs toward the heart. I am afraid he is dying by inches and that I cannot stop the progress of the cold. He begins to shiver every evening when the sun goes down. I pile on the blankets and turn up the thermostat but I cannot make him warm.

I am upset. I thought I had grown to hate him. But I do not hate him. I am beginning to see the logic of his flaws. I am beginning to see the easy ingratitude that has come to dominate my attitude toward him. Where, I ask myself, would I be today if it were not for Tellenbeck? *The meat safe*, I answer, and a bristling shudder moves down my spine.

In the evening, when the cold makes its greatest progress toward the heart, I cry by his bedside and ask him for forgiveness. I tell him that I will forgive him for his betrayal of trust if he will forgive me for my ingratitude. I tell him I understand his motives, his need for acceptance in the wary community of scientists. I beg him to try to understand my motives in imprisoning him like a beast. But he does not reply. Or, if he does, he replies to questions I have not asked.

"Tommy," he says. "It's your move."

They have taken me by the hand and pulled me toward her. I do not wish to go but I cannot resist them. *Well, well,* she says. They push me down and I fall upon her like an ax. *Rupture, rupture, rupture,* she says. Her voice is emotionless but her eyes are watching me with a sharp glint in them as if an unpleasant joke would soon be revealed. I am thrusting against her with limitless power. The others are clapping and murmuring the word *reveal* over and over. Then I explode. Then she splits. She splits all the way up. Her organs spill out over me and climb like tentacles. Their embrace is cold and wet. I see her face through a red mist. It is smiling with the usual satisfaction, though her eyes are turning up their whites with a new and covert pleasure, or with death.

"They fickle, Tom-Tom," says Tellenbeck. I am holding his hand. With my other hand I am drinking champagne out of the bottle and tapping red images out of my head. "They fickle, they gluppy, they burn," he says.

It is four A.M. and I am very tired, but the coldness is at his hips and at his shoulders. The thermostat is on ninety-nine and I have the electric blanket turned up to twelve. I am sweating, but Tellenbeck is blue with cold and chattering. His temperature is seventy-eight. His pulse is one hundred and sixty, when I can find it. He is paper white and his lips are daylight blue.

When the sun is high and the coldness recedes an inch, I take off his blankets and cut loose the bandage. The smell is sharp. It is difficult to suppress nausea. I am gagging, but holding back.

The wound has increased in size. The muscles have been tearing away under the pressure from within. The corium has followed suit and shows an ugly, jagged fissure. There is a great milky white bulging thing attempting to crawl out. I am tempted to pierce it, but this is not good medical practice. The sheets are foul with feces, urine, and blood. I run into the bathroom and vomit.

I come out of the bathroom, shaky and suddenly very tired. Then the feeling comes over me. I begin to laugh. Everything that is happening now has happened before. It is so clear and sharp I can taste it, like copper pennies. Tellenbeck opens his mouth and closes it. I know the word he is trying to form. I mouth it with him. He is rising up on his elbows, or attempting to, and trying to speak. He is watching me, looking at me as if for the first time. I fall down, paralyzed with mirth.

He dies. I watch death sweep over him like the passing shade of a cloud. It is evening and the fog has moved in. Lamps in the windows of other apartments glow like the yellow torches of a pilgrimage that is no longer moving. He lies there with his mouth slightly open, staring with an intense curiosity at the ceiling where the Fly scrubs his legs and preens.

There is nothing else to do and even if there were I am too tired and empty to do it. I open a bottle of champagne and turn on the TV. I plug in the tape of *The Invisible Man.*

I sleep. I wake. The screen is filled with visible noise. The bottle of champagne lies empty next to my chair. I rise and look in on Tellenbeck. He is still there, as is the Fly. I throw the bottle at the Fly but I miss by several feet. I go into the bathroom and look at myself in the mirror. My beard is several days long. I shave, taking great pleasure in the simple act. Then I take a hot bath.

I wrap Tellenbeck in the sheet and carry him into the workshop. I put him on the table. His remains no longer have the power to disgust. He is dry and crusty and sunken in on himself. I turn on the biosaw and render the body into small, easily manageable parts. I drop the parts into the emulsifier. I notice that the little finger of his left hand is crippled. The joints of the two knuckles

are *fused*. The rigid little finger stuns me. Tellenbeck
was a cripple! And I had never noticed! The discovery
touches me deeply and I must pause for several minutes
to recover the strength necessary to go on. I quickly
drop the remaining parts into the emulsifier, saving the
head for last. I hold it up and look into its cloudy eyes.
"Kraft," I whisper. "Kraft." I put my finger to the
slightly parted lips. I close each eye. I kiss the forehead.
Then I drop it into the emulsifier and kick the switch. In
minutes, what was Tellenbeck becomes cellglue. One
liter.

"THEY ALWAYS *look* innocent," says Chief Butz. "The
more innocent they look, the more suspicious you should
be." I am being reprimanded. Chief is angry. His face is
red and his thumbs are flicking. Two young men have
stolen six hundred dollars' worth of shoes.

"It's okay," they said. "There's been a sudden change
in fashion. We're taking out the old models."

Of course I did not believe this ridiculous story. I
knew what they were doing. But I could not bring myself to say *halt*. I put my hand on my weapon but they
did not notice. Their smiles were friendly and genuine.
Their faces were young and innocent even though they
were guilty. I opened my mouth and formed the word

halt but it would not come out. I watched them cross the mall and descend down the exit ramp to the parking plaza. There is something wrong, but I do not know what it is. I told Chief Butz the young men looked innocent, and it was not a fib.

I leave work early and go home. I tell Chief I am not feeling well. It is a fib. I do not know what is wrong. It is a weakness. But not of the muscles. In the apartment, I take off my uniform and give myself a quick physical. I am fine. There is no problem. I put on my sweat suit and go down to the weight room. I press three hundred and thirty pounds with ease. I am strong. I am not weak. There is no problem. I walk on my hands. I spring to my feet and jump high into the air. I touch my toes. I throw my shoulder into the wall. The building shakes. Something behind the wall falls. I am fine. I am strong. There is no problem.

I make an early supper. Cheeseburgers and champagne. My appetite is good. I eat three and drink a whole bottle. I feel better. I feel fine.

Then what is wrong?

If this is weakness, then where does it appear? I wheel around, suddenly, full-circle. A wariness makes the hair on my neck bristle. *What is it? Nothing.*

Then nothing is wrong. And there is no problem.

I fall into bed heavily. My heart is fifteen beats too fast. I hear its action. I rise and try to paint. I take out my old effort at self-portrait and make a few indecisive strokes. It is not a good canvas. I put my fist through it.

I break the frame. I crush the easel. I break my brushes. I empty my tubes of paint into the toilet. I return to bed.

I rise. I put on my uniform and strap on my weapon. I go out for a walk. The sky is brilliant and the air from The Green Sea is crisp. It is a fine afternoon. I walk down to the beach. I walk among the Sunbathers and gulls. The surf is high and booming like a TV war. The beach ends in a wall of huge stones. Stones like houses. I climb the stones until I reach the highest one. From this place I can see the entire beach, dotted with the colorful suits of the Sunbathers, the white buildings of the city shimmering to the south, the gray arms of the fog embracing the horizon. It is all very wonderful. There is no *reason* for weakness. Reasons for strength are all around me, far as the eye can reach. Reasons for strength fill my lungs with each breath. Reasons for strength warm the molecules of my skin, fill my nostrils with the sharp salt of The Green Sea, press with the inertia of granite against the soles of my shoes. No, there is no reason for weakness. There is nothing but reasons for strength, and there is no problem.

The thought of lying down on a flat rock and never rising enters my mind like a thief and I draw my weapon. "Move along," I say. The image of a bed floats before me and the urge to sleep numbs my spine. "No," I say. "Move along." I yawn. I bite my tongue. My eyes are suddenly heavy and stinging. I bite my tongue and step on my foot. "No!" I shout. I punch myself in the stomach and kick my ankle. "Move along!" I command. "Move along!"

I fire my weapon. The noise breaks up the luring thoughts and images of sleep. A gull explodes before my eyes on the rocks. Feathers are caught in the strong breeze and spiral around me. I fan them away from my face and shoot another gull and then another. The noise of the weapon makes me sneeze violently.

I walk on the beach holding the weapon before me and sneezing. Sunbathers rise and give me wide berth. I hear sirens in the distance. The memory of a torchlight search by angry villagers and Claude, desperate and alone in a dead-end boggy slough, sends shivers of terror through me. I holster my weapon and trot back to The Sun Spot, sneezing and sneezing, and keeping low, using streets I have not used before. When I am safe in my apartment, I take off my uniform and stand before the mirror. I sneeze. I give myself another physical. Systole one thirty-five, diastole ninety. I go to the refrigerator and swallow two handfuls of vitamins. I sneeze six capsules across the sink. I tilt the refrigerator and lift it several inches off the floor. I am fine. I am strong. And there is no problem.

Bully is autographing copies of his new book, *Spiritual Bugspray*. I am happy to see him again. He is dressed in a brown suit and is wearing a blue shirt with a white tie. I enter the bookstore and say hello to him. At first he does not remember. Then he, does. "Well, well," he says. "It's a rent-a-cop." He shakes my hand. "Say," he says, looking at my face. "You've picked up a tic or two, young fella."

I touch my face. "I have not been sleeping well," I tell him, and it is true.

"Par for the course," he says, signing a book for a murmuring, deformed man. When the man leaves, Bully leans close to me. "Look," he says. "I'm getting writer's cramp all the way up to the jowls. How about you and me sneaking off for a belt?"

It is against regulations, but I like the idea anyway. "There is a little place down the boulevard," I tell him.

Bully's car is a large, blue limousine. There are signs pasted on it. One says RADICAL HAPPINESS. Bully points to one that says HONK IF YOU'RE HUMAN. "No one honks," he says. He laughs. I laugh. His laugh is big. He does not hold it inside his body but lets it out until there is nothing in the world but his laugh. It makes me sneeze. Several people stop to watch this laughing and sneezing. Between sneezes I look at them through my dark glasses, letting my hand rest on the butt of my weapon, and they move along.

The bar is small but unoccupied. Bully orders gin. I order wine. "Euphoria," says Bully, raising his glass. "Radical happiness," I say, remembering the sticker on his car.

"So," Bully says. "You haven't been feeling well, is that it, Claude?"

I look at myself in the mirror behind the bottles. My

face is pale. "I feel fine," I say. "There is no problem."

Bully nudges me. "What about that tic? What about those bad nights?"

I feel fine. "I am as strong as two men," I say. I show him a muscle. It bulges in the gabardine sleeve.

Bully smiles. "Let me tell you a story about a man I heard of," he says.

Bully tells me a story about a man who was dying for no reason. The doctors were baffled. The man was only fifty, but he was wasting away and they could not stop this degeneration though they treated him with every known method of therapy. He lost weight. He could not eat. His sight and hearing were failing. He could not move his bowels. He slept fitfully and had bad dreams. The doctors gave up, finally, and said he had two or three more weeks to live. Then the man's wife called in another specialist. She had to sneak him into the hospital because he was known to the medical profession as a quack. The quack examined the dying man. After the examination, he said, "This man thinks his body is a Mixmaster. He thinks his body is a pile of gears, wheels, and levers. Moreover, this man loves his body less than he loves his electric shaver. This man has been snubbing his kidneys and sucking up to his Ford. This man has been treating his liver like an unwanted house guest." The quack then proceeded to talk to the man's internal organs. He had a little black horn. He put the bell of the horn against the man's body and spoke through the stem. "Hello, liver," he said. "This old boy been treating you poorly? Well, well, let's try to forgive and forget. Let's let bygones be bygones." He kept talking this way for quite a while. He talked to the kidneys, spleen, lungs, and stomach. He crooned to the large intestine. He sang lullabies to the bladder. It went on and on. A nurse overheard him and called in a doctor. The doctor had the quack evicted from the hospital over the protests of the dying man's wife, but it did not matter. The dying man had perked up. He sat up in bed and asked for a bowl of chili. He told his wife that he was feeling a lot better. In a few hours he was up and around.

"I'll never take my liver for granted again," he said. He left the hospital in two days. The doctors were amazed, but they saved face by telling everyone they saw that the man was a mental case to begin with and that all his problems had originated in his head.

"Of course," says Bully, "two highly regarded psychiatrists *had* given him a clean bill of health in that regard."

It is a good story. I like it. But I do not see how it applies to me. I do not take my body for granted. I tell Bully this. "Yes," he says. "But do you actively *love* your body? Picture your innards. Do you sweet-talk them?" That is foolish. But I say nothing. "See what I mean?" says Bully. "You're really no better off than that dildo in the hospital. You may think about your health a lot. You may be a bona fide hypochondriac, but unless you start giving some real credit to those workaday organs, why they're going to feel downright neglected."

I drain my third glass of wine. I am a bit annoyed by Bully's arguments. "Look," I tell him, suddenly reckless and angry, "I am a *monster*." I have forgotten that it is a pain word. The long nail rams my brain behind my right ear, but I do not wince. Bully looks at me closely. He raises his drink to his lips.

"All men are monsters," he says. "Trapped in a gumbo of flesh and bone."

I am gritting my teeth and holding back tears.

We do not speak for a while and the pain subsides. Then Bully says, "Sweet unstable machines."

I start to ask what he means and then decide to order another drink instead. I tap the bar three times and the bartender looks up from his newspaper. "Champagne cocktail this time," I say.

"When the monster sees that he is a sweet unstable machine," says Bully, "the spell is lifted."

I am interested in spite of the resurging pain. "What spell?" I ask through clenched teeth.

"The *evil* spell," he says. "Don't you get it, kid? The evil spell that turned us all into monsters in the first place, way back when." I bark with pain and pretend it is a cough but the tears are coming despite my efforts. I am remembering the disturbing Fable of the Frog Prince, the transforming cruelty of the selfish princess. I raise my glass and drink. The warming liquid scours my throat.

"Naarr," I say, tapping my skull with the heel of my

hand, the tears spilling down my face freely. *"Naarr."*

Bully laughs. He laughs long and hard. "Naarr," he says between bursts of laughter.

I begin to laugh too. The bartender hunches his shoulders and makes his hands into claws and limps back and forth behind the bar. We are all laughing very hard for no reason at all and saying *Naarr* when we can.

Among Tellenbeck's letters I find one from a Person named Manuel Marquez. The postmark says Caracas but the letter is written in English. The subject of the letter is something referred to as "the item." "The item" was to be sent to Mexico City by air express. From Mexico City it was to be transported to Guadalajara where it was to be picked up by a Señor Alvarado. Señor Alvarado was to take it by automobile to Guaymas. There, a Captain DeRaille would receive it aboard his trawler and transport it to the port of X. In a warehouse designated K–11, Tellenbeck would inspect "the item" and authorize, in the presence of Captain DeRaille, a Swiss bank to make four payments of five thousand dollars each to Manuel Marquez, over a period of twelve months.

In Tellenbeck's notebook, page one hundred and ninety-five, there is a single entry. "Twenty thousand dollars! It will break me! But if it is a fresh one—*not one cell damaged or deteriorated*—then worth every bloodsucking cent!"

Another letter from Marquez is written more informally:

Well, we had not the good fortune we had desired but after much diligence we found a satisfactory gentleman though he was some trifle unwilling, as you will readily understand, ha ha ha. Olé! But to the point: You requested an account of the details of "the acquisition" and I present them herewith. The "accident" was arranged by yours truly and his cousin by marriage, Gaspar the Fierce. Gaspar expressed a wish to enter the gentleman's premises with machetes flying! Olé! "We shall bring a *cubeta* of ice from the fish market," says Gaspar the Terrible, "slip into the bedroom and take 'the item' by force, pack it well in the *cubeta* and be gone." Presto! But with quick presence of mind, I labored to persuade my cousin, Gaspar the Bull, that his idea involved certain foreseeable risks. In effect, the family habitation offered an opportunity for ruinous complications that could easily be avoided by holding the "ceremonies" in a place less orchestrated to catastrophe. "Caramba!" says Gaspar the Quick, slapping his face and spitting into the wind. And so the true plan evolved. We spread large sheets of paper on the table in order to clearly outline and detail the superb elements of "the acquisition." (These sheets, you will be pleased to know, have since been returned to the elements from which they came, courtesy of your excellent Zippo Mfg. Co.) Gaspar the Fox, who works in the oil fields and contends that sixty percent of the world's misery is a direct manifestation of the Savior's indignation with the creation of the overland pipeline, suggests that we lure the gentleman into the mountains through vague appeals to his inborn *voracidad*. Arriba! Gaspar the Actor, disguising his voice to sound like that of a Norteamericano gangster, speaks guardedly of a secret uranium strike in the vicinity of El Tigre. "Dipsy Doodle!" says the gentleman, but Gaspar the Persistent makes him attentive with promises of easy riches and the return of Hispanic grandeur. To stamp the enterprise with the seal of authenticity, Gaspar the Fair speaks of a substantial financial contribution, which, however, shall be refunded in excess of ninety-five percent should the venture prove fruitless! The stroke and signature of a master! What could be at once hot and cold? To take with the left hand and to give back with the right! The dumbstruck *hombre* sneezed furiously on his snuff but agreed, at last, to a confrontation in the foothills of El Tigre prior to the placement of oaths on the paralegal *documentos*. The rest sleeps in the big sarape of history, with yours truly, and with my cousin by good fortune, Gaspar the Discreet.

¡Ai! ¡Cabronada! says a ragged and hopeless voice in my head. I see a small room with Females dressed in black and weeping. I strike myself on the forehead. I hear them sobbing. I slap my face. I hear a terrible sound and realize, amazed, that it is coming from my own throat. I punch myself in the jaw.

I am on the floor. It is dark. I do not know how long I have been lying here. I feel very weak. There is an insect buzzing in my ear. I rise and go into the kitchen. I swallow half a bottle of vitamins. I fix a small dinner and turn on the TV. There is a recent movie on the Late Show. I try to enjoy it. I try to eat. But it is useless. I cannot swallow.

I leave the apartment. It is foggy and cold outside. I

have put on the tuxedo jacket with the padded shoulders and the thick-soled shoes. The shoes hurt my feet and distort my walk. They make me lurch and sometimes stagger. I do not know why I decided to wear them. I look at my reflection in the large window of an apartment and am reminded of the stiff-legged creature in the hideous Karloff film which I have never recorded and never will though I watch it whenever it is on. "You are what you are," I say to the reflection, releasing a burst of wild laughter for no adequate reason at all.

I walk through the dark streets of the suburb. Occasionally a car passes me slowly, its passengers staring with open curiosity. I am the only walker. I walk, the clop-clop of my thick shoes echoing between the low bungalows and duplexes of this neighborhood. I walk, clopping so hard my feet hurt, toward the flaring lights of a boulevard.

I suddenly feel reckless and oddly free, but I do not trust the feeling because it is new and strange and involves the deliberate enjoyment of pain, such as the pain of these shoes, and the pain of seeing myself as others must eventually come to see me: grotesque, dangerous, *non-human*. I stop in a liquor store on the boulevard and buy two bottles of champagne and a bottle of brandy. The clerk spills my change on the floor behind the counter but I cannot wait for him to gather it and I leave while he is still on his knees. I open one of the bottles of champagne and the bottle of brandy. I sip the brandy and wash it down with the champagne. The warmth and the tickling bubbles are a welcome sensation in my throat.

The effect of the alcohol makes me exaggerate my walk. The stiffness of my legs rises into my hips and begins to travel up my spine. My neck is flexed and rigid as a stump and I am letting my lips flatten into an expressionless crease.

I am standing in front of a variety store. An idea occurs to me. I enter the store and purchase a pack of marking pencils. I take the pencils outside and, using the plate-glass window of a darkened restaurant, I draw melodramatic scars on my cheeks and forehead in reds, blues, and greens. It is very comical. I laugh and laugh and then I sneeze and sneeze. I take a sip of brandy and swallow the foaming champagne. There are people now, and some have stopped to look at me, their eyes large and startled. I let my lips snarl over my teeth and I roll my eyes with all the idiotic fury the gawkers expect. "Naarr," I say to them, lurching dangerously. Sometimes they walk swiftly away, sometimes they make obscene gestures, sometimes they laugh.

"Where's the party?" says a young Female in tall white boots.

"The party is over," I say to her, cryptically.

"So early?" she says.

"Everyone grew morose," I say.

"At a costume party?"

I raise my paper sack and sip the brandy. "The costumes were too good," I tell her.

"I know exactly what you mean," she says. "It was one of those Come-As-The-Character-You-Secretly-Want-To-Be parties and everyone got disgusted with everyone else."

"Exactly," I say, enjoying the silly fibbing banter.

"Sounds like a bunch of shitheels to me," says the girl, helping herself to my paper sack. "I'll be frank with you," she says. "I'm a hooker."

I know what that means. Luigi gives a little questioning nod hoping for the go-ahead, but I am not interested. "We could have a little party of our own up at my place. Looks like you've got plenty of booze there." She takes my hand.

"I . . . I do not think I am fit company tonight," I tell her.

"Well, we'll talk then. Sometimes that's all a man really needs or wants. Sometimes talking with a sympathetic woman is the best medicine."

I let her lead me along.

"For example," she says, "I am also pretty good at palmistry. I can sometimes tell a man just what he needs to know about himself. Getting crucial knowledge at a critical point in your life can be much more rewarding than, say, a blow job."

Her apartment is above a hardware store. It is small and poorly lit but quite comfortable. I sit on a faded couch. The Female, whose name is Iris Swette, brings two glasses. I fill them with champagne and lay an ounce of brandy on top. We clink glasses and drink.

Iris pats my thigh and Luigi jumps up like an undisci-
plined dog. "You sure you just want to talk?" she says,
an appealing slyness in her voice. I refill my glass.

"I am not sure of anything," I tell her.

She takes my left hand and looks at the palm closely.
I have a strong impulse to tell her everything now, without further delay. Everyone must know the truth, but I
must tell it to one Person at a time, and then it will
gather momentum and take on a life of its own and increase until it fills the entire world. "The line of Apollo
rises strongly from Luna," she says. "Smooth conic
fingers. Do you write poetry on the Q.T.?"

I shake my head.

"Oh oh," she says. "Health problems when you were
young, right?"

I laugh. "You might say so," I tell her.

"Hello, what's this?" she says. "A mystic cross?"

I withdraw my hand. "It is all nonsense," I say.

She takes my right hand. She looks, then looks again.
She takes my left hand and holds it beside the right. "I
don't get it," she says. "This is weird." I do not withdraw my hands. Let her discover what she must discover.
"My *God*," she says. "I've never seen anything like this!
They don't match!" She lets go of my hands and looks
at me. There is fear in her eyes. I drink it in, for this is
what I must prepare for. This is what I must learn to
embrace, this recognition of an impossible horror, this
terror, this sudden acceleration of distance between what
I know I am and what they believe themselves to be.

I rise and do the stiff-legged walk around her room. I
cock my head at a lunatic angle and say *Naarr* several
times letting my eyes roll and bulge. She is cowering in
a corner, edging for the door. I do not allow her to reach
it. I pick her up in my arms. She screams and then she
faints. I carry her into the bedroom and put her down
on the bed. She is thin, possibly undernourished, and
not very attractive. Her Tits are pathetically anemic.
There is a photograph of an elderly couple on her dresser.
On the wall, above the dresser, there is a large full-color
photograph of a child. I open her closet and look inside.
She has very few clothes, and what she has are of poor
quality. A tremor of pity relaxes the stiffness of my neck
and shoulders for a moment, but I shrug it off. I am in
no position to dispense pity. I pull the clothes from their
hangers and tear them to shreds. I walk around her
room, murmuring crudely, hands stupidly outstretched
in an excellent imitation of the Karloff travesty.

The girl stirs. I approach the bed, my hands moving
like claws in front of me. She opens her eyes. At first
there is nothing in them, and then they widen with recognition. I let my fingers touch her throat. "Oh no, Jesus,
please no," she says weakly.

"I am what I am," I say. I begin to close my fingers
on the quick pulse in her neck. She turns her head aside
and looks away. I see that she is looking at the photograph of the child on the wall.

I am touched by her acceptance of the inevitable. We
have both accepted the inevitability of the vulgar situa-

tion in which we find ourselves locked. I am deeply moved. I have never felt closer to another Person. As if she also feels the presence of this bond, she reaches up and touches my face.

I release her. "I am killing the wrong Person," I tell her softly. *Sí, bueno,* says the voice in my head, adding, in broken English, *It must be done.* I rise. She looks at me with confusion and guarded hope. I smile. I imagine my smile priestly and rich with illuminated benevolence. I take out my wallet and drop two twenty-dollar bills on the dresser, under the photograph of the child, and leave.

I walk home quickly, refusing to limp, lurch, or stiffen. My face is wet with tears, but they are not tears of pain or despair. The spotlight of an overhead helicopter locks on me for a moment, then passes on. Dogs and sirens howl in the suburb. A dozen rumbling motorcycles sweep darkly by. This is not my world.

This is not my world, I say over and over to myself, the tears coming now without restraint. I climb the hill toward The Sun Spot. I see that Connie's lights are on. But when I reach the door, I do not knock. Instead, I stand to one side of the large window and look in. There are several people sitting in a circle on the floor. Connie is talking to them. Their faces are struggling to understand what she is saying. They wear their frowns like masks. I watch Connie's lips and I know what she is telling them. I have heard her tell it before. *Think-er behind the think-er.* They lean forward and nod and smile with the satisfaction of discovery but their eyes are dull with confusion and Connie is looking at her watch.

No, not my world. I look up at the sky. The fog has dispersed and the night is sequined with other worlds, but none of them is mine either. I am out of place, and as long as I live, I always will be. I walk to the pool. The water is a black enamel rectangle. I step on the ladder and descend, breaking the glassy surface. This is the deep end of the pool, and I soon am submerged. When I reach the bottom, I sit down. The water is warm and pleasant. Soon I will have to breathe. And then I will take a single large breath and blackness will flood my brain, "the item" from Caracas, forever.

I have been speaking long and with passion in another language. I have been telling them about a wife and children. I do not understand the words, but the images and feelings that precede the words are clear. "*Perdido,*" I say, my voice hoarse and barely audible.

They are standing around my bed. A humming man is giving me an injection. Another is taking my blood pressure. The images and feelings recede gradually, and the strange words stop.

Marlene and Connie are rubbing my hands.

"*Claude,*" says Marlene.

"He'll be okay, ladies," says the man who has given me the injection.

"What was in that syringe?" I ask.

"I give you a dollop of B-one, man," he says. "Make

you feel like a tower of power. Make you want to boogie." The two men in white coats leave. They are carrying small medical bags.

"Who are they?" I ask.

"Paramedics from the Fire Department," says Connie. "We found you floating in the pool. Face up, thank heaven. What *happened*, Claude?"

I turn away from them. I now know that what they wish to know cannot be said. Nothing can or *should* be said. I pretend to sleep. But they do not leave. I pretend to snore. But they stay by my bed.

I pretend to dream. I am in the briar rose, careful of thorns, watching the giant's progress in the field. His stride is so long that as he walks away he shrinks by one-half his height with each step. One-half, one-fourth, one-eighth, one-sixteenth, one-thirty-second, one-sixty-fourth, yet he still seems huge and ominous to me, a dangerous fragment of evil on the horizon. And then he turns and comes back, growing by the same quick progression, until he towers over me like a thick, leafless tree.

I am very tired but I do not sleep. It is important that I remain awake. There is something short of death waiting for me at the bottom of sleep which must be avoided.

I have no strength. I try to flex my arms but the surge is not there. My fingers twitch in Marlene's hand. "Poor baby," she says. Connie is in the kitchen, making a broth. It smells good, but I know I will not have the strength to drink it. "When will your uncle be back?" Marlene asks. I try to shrug. The thought of Tellenbeck gives me pain and I cry but I am too weak to sob and the tears that fill my eyes do not sting.

"I have traded our cow for these magic beans, Mother," I say.

"Ai, picaruelo," she says. She takes the beans and throws them out the window. She does not know the wonderful consequences of this act, and so, in her despair, she beats me and weeps. *Mother, I am thinking, you have set everything in motion. Giants on the one hand, magical geese on the other.* Soon, she tires of beating me, and the blows soften into strokes.

It is a waking dream.

Connie brings the broth and turns on the TV set. Marlene holds my head and Connie puts the hot liquid to my lips. My mouth fills but I cannot swallow. The broth spills down the sides of my mouth.

They tuck me in. "We'll come back in the morning," says Connie. "Meanwhile, you get a good night's sleep." They place the remote-control device for the TV in my hand and leave.

I switch through all the channels aimlessly. The faces and gestures bore. The music and gunfire bore. I turn on the weather channel and watch the barometer. Twenty-nine point nine and falling.

I did not leave my bed today. I am not hungry. In the

evening I try to think of food. I imagine a nice steak. I think of steaming rolls, a platter of fresh corn. Nothing stimulates saliva.

I rise and there is a weakness that reaches deep into the muscles and touches bone. I am startled, but not frightened. I roll out of bed. I crawl to the dresser and pull myself up. I stand. I walk, leaning on furniture and trembling.

It is dark in the apartment. I dwell in darkness and prefer it. An image of the dark rectangle of the swimming pool at night under the stars occurs to me often. I see it smooth and opaque, without depth, a mirror for the infinite emptiness above.

The string is tied around my wrist. If the wrist falls, the light is switched on, and I awake. I will allow myself to doze, but I will not permit sleep. When the wrist falls and the light startles me awake, I rise and go into the bathroom. I stare at myself in the mirror while the cold water runs over my hands.

My face is turning gray. The flesh sags beneath the skin and the skin is without resilience.

Connie and Marlene come and go. They appear to be nervous and worried. They have offered to call in a doctor, but I have refused. "I will be all right," I tell them, though it may be a fib.

I have lost track of days. Marlene tells me she has called Chief Butz and has placed me on sick leave. I do not care. I will not return to the Security Force. I do not care if they steal the shoes and call it a sudden change in fashion. I do not have the interest to say, *You there, Move along,* or *Halt.* Let them steal.

Today the little toe of my left foot fell off. I stubbed it against a dresser as I was crossing the room. There was little pain though the blow was severe. I looked down. The little toe had rolled under the dresser. I picked it up and looked at it. The wound was glistening pink but there was no flow of blood. For the first time in days I am frightened. But this fear is unlike the fear of times past. There is a separation in my mind. There is a gulf between myself and the emotion, between the thinker and the feeler, as Connie might say. It is almost Someone Else's fear. Yet I know it is mine. I see my hands trembling. I hear my heart rattle the bones of my ear. I see the desperation in my eyes. I feel the dryness of my throat.

I go into the workshop and open the emulsifier. I take an eyedropper of cellglue. I spread the clear paste on the little toe and reattach it to my foot. I bandage the area tightly and hope for the best.

I return the unused cellglue to the emulsifier. "Thank you, Doctor Tellenbeck," I say.

For he is the glue.

Marlene is with me, scolding. "I'm not going to stand by while you shrivel up into a pathetic shut-in!" She bathes me with warm soapy water. She gives me a massage. It does not feel good or bad. I am indifferent to her hands. It exasperates her. She takes Luigi and kneads him. I try to protest. I try to make my face look fierce. I think of the Giant's twisted face, how horrible it must look, and I try to imitate it. I remind her of the broken chairs. "Go ahead, Claude," she says. "Break a chair. Do it." I cannot rise. But neither can Luigi. There is sensation. A remote tingling, a distant urge, a spidering squib of voltage, but that is all. I close my eyes.

Her hands give me waking dreams. They rise up like bubbles in heavy oil, slow and torpid, rainbowed with images that have a transitory interest, and when they reach the surface they linger momentarily, then burst.

I watch the weather channel. Sometimes I watch Claude Rains, but only in fragments. The whole drama fatigues me. I watch him wrap himself in bandages. I watch the rage of the village. But I mainly watch the dials and meters of the weather channel.

The barometer reading is low. Twenty-nine point two and falling. A wind from The Green Sea has started to blow. I can hear it buffeting against the apartment. I can see its velocity on the screen. Twenty-five knots and rising. Small-craft warnings have been posted. It is inadvisable to begin a long journey with a trailer in tow.

Do not fly. Do not plan an outing. Check your weather stripping. Tie down your light equipment. Check your drainage.

I am awakened from a mild doze by an explosion. I

have never heard such a noise. My heart is beating high in my chest and fast. The wind is howling at the window. The sky is black. Then everything is illuminated by a blue electrical discharge. Another terrible explosion follows. "Tellenbeck!" I shout, but it is not much more than a whisper. "*Kraft!*" I see the sky webbed suddenly with jagged blue lines and a fireball flares at the top of a TV antenna. The explosion is immediate and the bed jumps.

I turn on the TV but there is nothing on the screen but a rain of sparks. Crashing static from the loudspeaker hurts my ears.

I sink back into bed and pull the covers over my head.

The Fly preens in a bright patch of sunlight on the ceiling directly above my face. A large bearded man in a brown suit is looking at me. He would like me to look at him. But I cannot take my eyes from the Fly. Should he move, should he take a new position behind my head where I could not see him, I would be seriously distressed.

"We found him under the blankets, stiff as a board," says Marlene. I see her as a blaze of red and white off to one side. I hear Connie moving in the kitchen.

"Is that so?" says the bearded man affably.

The bearded man shines a light into my eyes. "Ha ho," he says. He begins to hum. I recognize the tune. It is from the coda of a mediocre symphony. He touches his nose with his thumb. He pushes his nose slightly to one side and rubs it. He closes his eyes and frowns. He takes a deep breath and clears his throat. He sneezes into his wrist. He takes a nail file out of his jacket pocket and takes a rough edge from his thumbnail. "Dream of wood?" he asks, in an offhand manner. "Dream of paper?" He is busy with his thumbnail and I am not sure he is asking these questions of me. In any case, I cannot speak. "Chests? Bottles? Jars? Caves? Pits? Coffers? Ships? Tables? Cups? Bowls? Books? Drawers? — *Mouths?*" But I cannot move my lips. And I must keep my eyes on the Fly. While I am watching him, he will not move. This is my understanding of the situation. "Well then," says the bearded man, still filing his thumb. "How about guns? Knives? No? Swords? Nails? No? Hammers? Pencils? Pens? No? Shoes? Fingers? Toes? Strike a nerve? No? Snakes? Necks? Fountains? Getting warm? No? Balloons? Zeppelins? Airplanes? Yes? Airplanes? Perhaps in these nutty little movies *you* are the airplane? Ha ho? I am getting warmer? Yes? No? Are you the airplane?" He stops filing his thumbnail and leans close to me. His face is inches from mine. "You know," he says, whispering, "you're not fooling me for a minute, you big son of a bitch." Then he sits back until his face is out of range and begins to file another nail. "I am reminded," he says, in a needlessly loud voice, "of a similar case some years ago. The patient in question happened to be a female photographer for the Department of Highways. Now, as you must know, everything pathogenic in the unconscious is eventually kicked upstairs to the conscious mind, no two ways about it. Very well, then. *Il y a fagots et fagots*, to quote the famous old Frog. What I knew about her, she did not choose to understand. What she knew about herself, I did not choose to believe. *Impasse, mon frère? Mais non!* The narcissistic neuroses are the easiest nuts to crack! You see, she was compulsively destroying exposed film, the symbolic content of this act being quite obvious, of course, even, I am afraid, to the female in question herself! Ha ho! Yes? You see what I am driving at? Well. It threw me off the track. Off-the-track! You see? She wasn't, what you might call, *cooperative*. Ha. Not one bit. I paced and I paced. I wrangled, pardner! Lens-film, eye-mind. You see my train? The appropriation of *life* itself, through the peephole, in collusion with the eye, the mouth of the mind. Suffering voyeurs! A set of gripping sphincters so parsimonious she probably shit nothing but beebees. The secret lascivious appetite, the old story, and holy moley, how sick I am of hearing it! *But wait*, I told myself. *Too easy, too easy, professor. Trop académique, mon cher.* I went through half a box of surrogate Cuban ropes before it hit me. Her daddy, you see, had this glass eye. I had it in my notes someplace or other. Didn't think much of it at the time. Glass eye, big deal. I've had them come in with neoprene assholes. Vaginas lined with Reynolds Wrap. Jock straps stuffed with Farina. You name it, dad, I've seen it." He puts his nail file away and signals to Marlene. "Anything to drink in this dump, sis?" he asks. Marlene goes out and brings him a glass of Riesling. I can smell it. "Well then," he says, making a face at the drink, but smacking his lips. "They had this game going, *Catch the Eye*. Papa would pretend to doze in his rocker, newspaper on his lap, while the daughter played dolls by the big radio. 'Whoops!' Papa would say, and that was the signal for the daughter to drop her dolls and dive for Daddy's chair, usually just in the nick of time to catch the flying eye. Sometimes she'd make a one-handed grab just before it hit the linoleum. Other times she'd get it on the first bounce. But that wasn't the fun part. The fun part came next. The little dickens would then climb up on Daddy's lap and rein*sert* the eye in its socket. Daddy would put his head back on the cushion and give her instructions. 'A little to the left. Not too hard. Press, don't shove.' Generally it would take her ten to fifteen tries to get it in right. Beginning to get the drift? Little girl working that glass nubbin into the old boy's head, the old boy lying back and creaming his denims. Some game, huh? Bonkers, my friend, bonkers. What threw me off at first was her dreams. Claimed she dreamed her soul was imprisoned in a daguerreotype. Claimed she walked on a misty heath searching for her imprisoned soul. Claimed she saw her face in the clouds, sailing away toward Araby. What a crock! She had me jotting down that junk for months. Cost her plenty, though. But we sure as hell weren't getting anywhere with her costly little habit of wrecking state property until she squared with me."

Marlene refills his glass and he drinks it down in one swallow. "Hey, don't get the idea I'm a wino, ginger," he says, patting her on the thigh. Then he leans toward me again. "Some weird crapola, eh paisan? I mean that business about the glass eye. Thought you'd heard it all, eh fella? Ha ho?" He squeezes my arm hard and stands up. He looks at his watch. "Got to split," he says. "Got this mother who thinks his dork is a yam. Got to enlighten the chump. Thinks his mom's got her eyes on it for the holidays."

To Marlene he says, in a confidential voice that I can hear clearly, "Get a hundred simoleons to my office by Friday and I'll be back on Monday, okay? But just between you and me, cookie, that big stupe is faking it, right down the line. Guys with bods like that don't fall apart so easy. They don't fall down and play dead, kid. It just doesn't happen. You know, he reminds me a lot of Steve Reeves in *Hercules Unchained*. Especially his pecks. *Clean*. Ever catch that flick? Steve is my fave." He unbuttons his jacket. "I do a little body-building myself, you know." He unbuttons his shirt. I see, out of the corner of my eye, a rippling of pink flesh. "I can make my pecks do the rhumba," he says. "You could scrub out your undies on my abdominals, sis."

If I keep my eyes on the Fly, he will not move. That is my understanding. I no longer need to sleep. I do not doze. I lie here wide awake, hour after hour, watching. Yet, I dream. I often dream of Tellenbeck. He appears to me as he did in the beginning. Kind and generous, watchful and good. "You've really mucked things up, Claude," he says. I have to agree. He has brought me a tray of snacks. Endive on whole wheat. Ginger ale. He sits on my bed and we watch a movie together. "I suppose," he says, "it's just as much my fault as it is yours. I never should have allowed you to think of yourself as a Person. I should never have allowed you to name yourself Claude, after that tired old actor. What do you see in him anyway?" It is not possible for me to answer. "I should have insisted on Alpha Six, all along," he says. "Never should have allowed myself to lose sight of the *experiment.*"

Sometimes I dream of the giant Female and the magic goose. We talk in her kitchen. She tells me that the Giant is away on urgent business. "Well," she says, "what shall we do to while away the hours?" I do not know. I am holding the magic goose on my lap, stroking its soft down. The giant Female takes out a deck of cards and deals two hands. We play a game. Not until she says "Gin!" and spreads her arms like wings do I see that her Tits are loosening. She sees me noticing the catastrophic diapause and retrogression and closes her arms on her chest. Her scars gradually reappear, like images on a film immersed in developing fluid. Her mouth grows thin and downcast. Her eyes cloud with anger and resentment. I hear the Giant chuckling crudely and wheezing behind the briar rose, the long hiss of his sickle.

Sometimes I dream of the fog. It fills the room. The

sun squibs green and cold in the center of the fog. I hear the slap of waves against the bed. A gray gull knifes through the ceiling. Its eyes are black and lusterless. It speaks my name. It makes a noise like a dry hinge.

Sometimes I dream of painting. Sometimes it is a self-portrait. I paint a white oval surrounded by murk. I stand back, unable to give the oval features. Then I cut out a photograph of Claude Rains and paste it on the oval.

Sometimes I dream I am in another country. I am loved here and there is a celebration being held in my honor. There is dancing and singing. Speeches are being made on behalf of friendship and fidelity. A Female in a dark room in singing for light, and it comes. The Female calls to me. *Carlos,* she says, and I enter her. We move together as we always have, in an old and familiar way. Somewhere there is the sound of children laughing. A distant guitar celebrates the idea of inevitable solitude. Holding each other, always as if for the last time even though our future is unclouded, we cry. We caress one another delicately, sensing the impermanence. She touches my Luigi and I do not forbid it. The Luigi is normal. Human.

I HEAR a Female reading softly to herself. Another Female is dusting the furniture. The Female dusting is elderly and very small. My peripheral vision is good. Though I must not take my eyes from the Fly, I can see most of the activity in the room. I can almost see the door. When someone enters, I see the opening and closing, the vague shape approaching. My hearing is more than adequate. Someone is in the kitchen making a pot of coffee. The Fly is preening.

"So, he just lies there like that?" asks the small, elderly Female as she dusts.

"Yes," says the reading Female. It is Connie. She closes her book.

"Anybody asked him why?"

"He doesn't talk."

"Does he sleep?"

"We don't know."

"Move bowels?"

"No. But then he doesn't eat anything either."

"Hmmm. You go on home, hon. Pa and me have to talk about this."

I see Connie rise and go. She does not speak to me. I wish that she would even though I cannot meet her eyes or respond.

The Fly will sometimes buzz and lift his head, though he cannot leave, as long as I remain motionless and do not sleep. It is a contest. Soon, for lack of food and movement, one of us will have to break off. I do not think I can win. And yet, it is the Fly that seems most impatient. I smile inwardly with this notion. I have patience. If it were possible, I could wait forever. The Fly is impatient because he is rapacious and stupid. His mind serves one end. From within my immobility, I jeer at him. I may lose the contest, but the victory will be mine. This thought almost lets me close my eyes. But the following thought of unguarded sleep in which the Fly sucks my existence from the corners of my eyes, or enters my ear to touch the brain, or perhaps hides himself within my nose, frightens me alert again. I must increase my vigilance, though my confidence is rising. Vigilance must be increased as a *consequence* of rising confidence. This paradox interests me and so I follow it up. I reduce it to an abstract principle and test it in a wide variety of possible situations. My mind is alert and healthy. The paradoxes multiply. I see them as metaphysical atoms, composing the human universe. It is a universe to which I add myself, even though I know better.

They are old and small. The Female is no more than five feet tall. The old man is not much more than that. They stand by my bed and look at me. Serious questions are etched in the lines and hollows of their faces. "Where is Kraft, young man?" asks the elderly Female. "We are his parents," says the old man.

Each day, several times a day, they stand by my bed and ask this question.

Each time the elderly man says *We are his parents*, I feel a surge of amazement and hope. I am amazed that I knew nothing of Tellenbeck beyond our immediate relationship. He was the genius responsible for me. That was all I knew. That was enough. The idea that *he* had parents, that others were responsible for *him*, amazes me. And oddly fills me with an expansive hope I cannot explain.

"You were his friend, and you got sick," says Tellenbeck's mother. It is half a question, half a statement. "What's it look like to you, Father?" she says to her husband.

"Snakebite," says the old man. "Though he may be touched some."

"If only we had some *Blutreinigungsmittel*."

"To thin his blood some."

"Or some *Schwitzgegreider*."

"To perk him up."

"Maybe we should find a *Brauch*."

"To kick his butt."

"Papa," says the old Female. "You go, I stay. You get the sassafras and burdock. You can get chamomile at the store, but go to the hills we came through east of here and see if you can find the mugwort and feverfew. I'll pack you a lunch."

"We'll fix it, boy," says the old man to me. "We'll make you sweat and puke."

"We'll make him a poultice," says the Female.

"We'll make him shit, Mama."

"We'll warm you up, son."

"You'll be chewing your fingers and asking for orange juice in no time."

"A quart of aqua vitae to make him holler."

"To clean his blood."

"Invigorate his bones."

"We're simple people, boy."

"Our philosophy is, if it don't work, fix it. If it won't be fixed, bunch it."

"We're farmers."

"If what comes up out of the ground can't put you right, then you can't be put right."

"City folks like to call it mumbo jumbo."

"That's why they're all sick as cats."

"That's why they don't sleep, eat good, or shit on a regular basis."

When the old man leaves, the old Female sits by my bed and watches my face. She leans toward me and looks closer. Her eyes are large and young looking. Her ears are long and fleshy. "Something ain't right about you that don't have a thing to do with your sickness," she says.

Another time she says, "You just ain't staring off into empty space, are you, boy?" She is so close to my face I can feel her breath. "You're looking *at* something," she says. She follows my gaze to the ceiling. She takes out a pair of ancient wire glasses and puts them on, hooking them carefully over her large ears. She squints up at the ceiling.

The Fly becomes tense and alert. He stops his endless preening. He flexes his legs.

The old Female is agile. She stands on her chair and

squints hard in the direction of the Fly. His legs flex down a little lower. She steps from the chair to the bed, which brings her closer to the ceiling.

"Kraft used to come home every summer for years," she says to me, but still squinting up at the Fly. "When it was time to hay, Kraft would run the baler. Or the mower. And he'd help put it up." She raises her right hand slowly and cups it behind the Fly. "Then he got his fancy education and we haven't seen him but half a dozen times in twenty-five years." She brings her left hand up in front of the Fly. The Fly is rigid. "We were beginning to forget what he looked like. So we decided to come down here. But all we found was a sick boy in Kraft's apartment who won't talk." She opens her left hand and moves it slowly toward the Fly. "The world is full of tricks," she says, making a slow, slapping pass at the Fly with her left hand.

The Fly is filled with contempt for her feeble effort. He rises heavily, expecting to land a few inches away. But then her right hand, which had been cupped behind the Fly, well past his vision, snaps forward like a trap. I see the bony old hand blur on a limber wrist. I see it snap shut. On the Fly.

She steps down from the bed carefully. I am still staring at the ceiling where the Fly had been, but it is uniformly empty. She holds her right fist next to my ear. I hear a muted buzz. "That what you were staring at, boy?" My mouth, which had been dry, suddenly fills with saliva and I choke. "Now we're getting somewhere," she says.

"You *saw* it?" I say, though my lips barely move. She holds her fist next to my ear again. The buzz is wild with rage. The little old Female smiles. She goes into the bathroom. I hear the toilet flush. She comes back into the bedroom.

"City flies are filthy things," she says, brushing her hands against her dress.

Klaus and Trude have made me well. Klaus is Tellenbeck's father and Trude is his mother. They are in their eighties but they are vigorous and alert. They have purged me with herbs and poultices. Trude made dissolved beef for me so that my strength would return. The meat had to be boiled for twelve hours, strained and chilled. She spooned it into my mouth. She believed the action of my heart was weak and so she gave me black cohosh, skullcap and lobelia. She gave me dandelion root and catnip for my stiffness. She pinned a charm on my pillow for good luck. She told me that worry, fear and resentment clog up the bloodstream with impurities. She gave me garlic juice and told me to think about the Garden of Eden and the absence of corruption, injustice, and chemical food. I did.

I lost weight during my illness but even so I feel wonderful. I am not as strong as I was, but I am strong enough. I do not think I can press three hundred pounds, but I think I can press two hundred and fifty. But I do not go down to the exercise room to find out.

I have called Chief Butz and told him that I will not return to the Security Force. He did not ask why and I did not tell him.

I will look for other work, but I am in no hurry.

I take long walks and try to sort things out. My mind is placid and efficient. I am grateful to Klaus and Trude.

I walk with a limp. The little toe that fell off is sore now and healing slowly. Twice I have taken off my sock and the toe was still in it. I use more cellglue and hope for the best.

The other day, Klaus was looking around the apartment. He went into the workshop. He looked at the machines. They meant nothing to him. Then he opened the emulsifier. "Smells like rancid peanut butter in there," he said.

I could not bring myself to tell him the truth. How could I say, *This small vat of thick fluid is your son?* "It is an organic binding agent made of peanut oil," I said, fibbing.

"Glue?" he asked.

"Yes," I said. "Glue."

"Kraft was always fooling around with his chemistry set," he said, absently.

"Kraft is a genius," I said.

"I know. That's what he always used to tell us."

Klaus and Trude have not told me how long they intend to wait for Tellenbeck to return. They do not seem impatient. They do not seem especially curious about me and what my relationship is to their son. I have planned to tell them that I am his laboratory assistant, but so far there has been no need to do so.

They spend their mornings at the kitchen table drinking black coffee and talking to each other in low, almost secretive, voices. In the afternoon they go for a stroll on the beach. In the evening they watch TV until nine. They drink another cup of coffee, speaking in those confidential half-whispers, and then, at ten, they go to bed. They sleep in Tellenbeck's room. They fall asleep quickly and they snore. The snores begin immediately and increase in strength until, by midnight, their combined breathing sounds like a small gasoline engine. They sleep this way until five. At five, Trude rises and makes a pot of coffee. Klaus rises next. He shaves and dresses and goes out into the kitchen where his coffee is waiting for him. I have adopted their habits. We sit in the kitchen, drinking coffee. They speak softly to each other, but I do not feel excluded. Sometimes when there is a pause, I make a comment about something interesting I may have noticed out the window. A cloud formation, for example. They listen to me and respond with intelligence and often with insight. I like being with them very much. I almost tremble with pleasure, anticipating my first cup of morning coffee.

Sometimes we speak of our dreams. "I dreamed I was locked in the barn and it had begun to rain," says Klaus.

"All our hay was still in the field."

Trude chuckles at this and shakes her head. "He can't leave home for a day without getting the heebie jeebies."

"So, enough is enough," says Trude. We are sitting in the kitchen drinking our evening coffee. It is nearly ten P.M.

"That's for sure," says Klaus. "Grain is likely headed by now."

I have invented an elaborate story about how I thought Tellenbeck had decided to travel to South America and investigate some new developments in molecular biology at a private research clinic in Buenos Aires. I described the correspondence he has had with an important research scientist by the name of Manuel Marquez. But they did not seem interested in the fibs. Sometimes they look at me with their pale eyes and it is as if they see the exact truth of the situation and I have to turn away and pretend that what they appear to see is not there but only in their minds.

"We could use a strong boy like you, Claude," says Klaus, "if you're interested in a lot of hard work for hardly any pay." He laughs. It is a crackling, brittle laugh. Trude laughs too. Her laugh is musical and young. Then they are looking at me again in that searching, solemn way, and I turn aside, pretending they see nothing, or that if they do, it is a mistake. "Personally," says Klaus, "I don't see how you city people can stand it here.

Years ago we'd read these picture stories of how things would get to be, with all those glass towers and auto-gyros flitting around like June bugs, the people dressed up like lunatics. Seemed like a thousand years off. And now here it is. But it isn't like anyone figured. People feeling more and more left behind and stupider by the minute."

Trude touches Klaus's hand. "Now, Pa," she says.

"People turning themselves inside out to be as dumb as their machines," he says.

"Now, Pa," Trude says.

Before they leave, Klaus shows me his map. "You take the blue highway here across the desert and over to this intersection with the green highway. Take the green highway north until you start to climb up into these mountains. They are called the Aurora Mountains by most folks. Now when you get to this little gray, broken-line road, turn right on it. Stay on it until you reach this black river. It's called Purgation Creek, though the maps will sometimes call it Temptation Creek, depending, I guess, on which way you're coming from. Anyway, you cross it, and then after another mile or so you come to a pair of little two-rut roads. Take the left fork, which isn't on the map. Go ten miles and you'll be on our property. Go another two miles and you'll see our house. Red with white shutters under the biggest elm tree in the world. You decide to come up, we'll put you in Kraft's old room, just like one of the family. Do you good."

❦

THE PARTY is for Zip and Marlene. They are going to get married. It is a large party that begins in Connie's apartment and spills outside to the patio and around the pool. There are musicians. There are tables of food. There is an old bathtub filled with red punch. I am sipping from a glass of ginger ale, and watching. I am well, I am strong, but I do not feel able to participate in this celebration. I am enjoying the party, I am happy for Marlene and Zip (the Someone Else who sometimes rages senselessly about their relationship has not intruded upon my thoughts), but my pleasure is strictly that of a spectator. I have purchased new clothes for the party and for my trip. I am wearing a charcoal black wool suit and a green turtleneck pullover. My shoes are white suede with three-inch heels. I am wearing wrap-around sunglasses and my hair glistens with fragrant oil.

My size seems to startle many of the guests and they do not talk to me for very long after the introductions. Fine. I am in no particular need of conversation. *Well, what is your line, Mr. Rains?* Staying alive. They chuckle nervously and they leave. *What are you drinking, pal, soda pop?* I am drinking ginger ale. I have come to believe that alcohol is what causes my little toe to fall off every time I turn around. *Oh, is that so?* they say, and they leave.

A Female insists that I dance with her. She is intoxicated and her hair is flying. Her Tits are easily visible and she presses them into my wool jacket. "Ooh, scratchy," she says. She is swaying erratically. I am holding her and moving my feet stiffly backward and forward, worried about the dysfunctioning toe. One two. One two. Luigi is slow to react but he finally begins to butt her thighs. "Hey, cool off," she says, her face losing its drunken look.

I go out to the patio. Silhouettes of swaying people merge with the darkness. I bump into a fat man. "Nothing changes except the time of day," he says, wearily. It is Bully. I am happy to see him.

"I want to give you something," I say. I take him up to my apartment. I give him the painting called *Full Moon over Solar Flats*. He is grateful and appreciative of my skill.

"I'll hang it in the café," he says, "behind the counter where it'll be noticed by the rubes." He looks through my other canvases. "Hey," he says. "I'll *buy* this one from you." It is a portrait of Trude and Klaus. I had purchased a new set of oils and painted it from memory. They are seated at the table, their small hands touching, their heads close together in quiet conversation.

"No," I say. "It is meant for another."

Bully holds up a third canvas. It is clear blank blue. Solid sky, from border to border. "What's this supposed to be?" he asks.

"I call it *Portrait of the Artist*," I say. Bully looks at

me, sees that I am smiling, then slaps his thigh and laughs and laughs until I sneeze.

We return to the party. I do not wish to stay much longer but Connie and Marlene are my friends. I have brought a painting for Connie. I look for her in the roaring party but I do not find her. I see that her bedroom door is slightly open and that the light is on. I peek inside and Connie is sitting on the bed giving counsel, it appears, to a man in a motorcycle helmet. "So they adopted me," the man is saying, "knowing what it would mean to me later on." The man's voice is bitter though he is trying to laugh. "And it was *great*, Connie. I had a great childhood. They spoiled me rotten. Then one day, don't ask me why, I walked in on Mom while she was taking a shower. I was twelve years old. It destroyed me." He puts his face in his hands and Connie pats him on the shoulder. "Suddenly I understood their little joke, their little sweet-talk. 'Going up the old dirt road tonight, doll?' Mom would say to Dad across the dinner table. Dirt road? Dirt road? We lived in the city. What did she mean *dirt road*?" A ragged sob shakes his shoulders. "These two homos living together as man and wife, buggering the dogturd out of each other for years, and me thinking everything was *cool*. My God, Mom was the den mother for my Cub Scout pack!" He blows his nose. He wipes his tears with the sleeve of his leather jacket. "I pulled back the shower curtain that morning and there was this little blue dick staring me in the eye. Surprise, junior! And do you know what I did?" Connie pats his hand and shakes her head solemnly. "I said, 'Sorry, Mom,' and ran out. And for the next six years, up to the time I joined the paratroopers, I pretended everything was normal. I pretended there was nothing unusual up Mom's skirt. And of course the two of them went right along with the act. 'Going up the old dirt road tonight, doll?' Jesus! God, how I dreamed of cutting their throats in their rotten bed! In fact, I still *do!*" He breaks down and begins to cry without restraint. Connie puts her arms around him.

"There, there," she says. "You've had a hard time of it, haven't you?"

I clear my throat. They look up at me. I see a flicker of annoyance cross Connie's face before she smiles. Her smile is genuine, but it is distant. I am embarrassed. I should not have intruded. "I am sorry," I say, bowing slightly from the neck and saluting. "I just wanted to leave this with you before I go." I put the picture down and lean it against the wall. It is a painting of Jake the gorilla. He is looking up at the viewer, and through him.

I LEAVE early and head east on the blue highway. All I have with me is the painting of Klaus and Trude, my self-portrait, my jonquil bulbs, my clothes, and six thermos bottles filled with cellglue. The thermos bottles ride on the seat next to me. They rattle and click with the vibrations from the highway and I speak to them. "Home, Kraft," I say to the silver cylinders. "We are going home." And it is not a fib. It is where Tellenbeck started and therefore it is where I started. And so it is where we must return. No one started in The Sun Spot. It is a place where one may end, if one is unfortunate, but it is not a place where one can start. Once I thought it was a place of great beauty, much like the magical landscape of the Beanstalk, but now I do not. My seeing has steadily improved.

I drive very fast. I keep the speedometer on eighty when the highway is empty. Sometimes I feel as though I am running away from something malignant. Other times I feel as though I am trying to reach something elusive, something that will disappear if I am not quick enough or sufficiently ardent. Wind and weather do not slow my progress. When I am tired I pull off the road and lie down in the back of the van and doze for ten minutes. During these brief naps, I dream vividly of a wild country, beyond the castle of the Giant and his magic goose. When I awake I am filled with fear. Fear that I have dozed too long and that what I am running from has gained on me or that what I am running toward has receded. In these moments I almost can hear the heavy footsteps of catastrophe crushing the pavement behind me. When I reach the intersection of the blue highway and the green highway, the feeling of urgency doubles. I no longer stop to doze ten minutes. I drive continuously and at very high speeds. My hands are cramped and stiff from holding the wheel. Sometimes I imagine I can see small fissures appearing around the knuckles. I shudder, but I do not relax my grip. In my fatigue, I sometimes can feel fissures spidering all over my body, and in my face. A picture of sudden retrogression rides before me out on the highway, like a ghost of the future. I see myself splitting, a transparency in the windshield gliding over the pavement, the Fly moving busily in the bleeding cracks.

I stop in a small town and find a drugstore. I buy all the rolls of bandages they have. The clerk becomes curious. "Expecting an accident?" he asks, grinning.

"If I disintegrate," I tell him, "I will not be able to see myself." He looks at me a long moment and then decides to laugh, but his laugh is meant to hide a sudden, alarming notion.

I climb in the back of the van and wrap my legs carefully. They feel much better this way. The flesh cannot split. The arteries cannot rupture. I wrap my torso and then my arms. The organs cannot explode if they are held in by layers of strong gauze. I wrap my hands, leaving only the thumbs exposed.

I wrap my head, allowing slits for my eyes, nose, and mouth. I put on my dark glasses, and a cap. I pull the collar of my jacket high around my neck. I drive.

I feel safe. I feel invulnerable.

I feel like Claude, moving through the countryside, beyond the rage and fear of the villagers. Beyond their tricks and bad dreams. And almost home.